Twisted Knickers

A Bunch of Shorts (Stories)

Robert Hart

Twisted Knickers

A Bunch of Shorts (Stories)

Robert Hart

published by

Cover art by Chris Holmes of White Rabbit Graphix.

ISBN# 978-0692728376

I am Oliver, and I am a Cat first appeared in FWA Collection, Volume 1, *From Our Family to Yours,* page 115; Guest Editor, Author of Renown: Suzette Martinez Standring. Peppertree Press, 2009.

Inheritance first appeared in FWA Collection, Volume 5, *It's a Crime,* page 5. Guest Editor, Author of Renown: Michael Wiley. Peppertree Press, 2013. **(# 1 Choice)**

Two first appeared in FWA Collection, Volume 7, *Revisions,* page 90; Guest Editor, Author of Renown: Marie Bostwick, Black Oyster Publishing, 2015 **(Highest judges' score.)**

Twisted Knickers
A Bunch of Shorts (Stories)

Don't get your knickers in a twist: Don't get upset over something you have no control over.

My wife thought the title too suggestive, so I told her there was a sub-title, *Screwed-up Shorts.* She looked at it, looked at me, and said, "What did I tell you?" I changed it to '*A Bunch of Shorts.*' Perhaps I shall use the Latin alternative. "*Non torsii subligarium!*"

Most of these stories I call Frivolettes, short pieces of no deep or lasting literary merit. They cover a range of expression from the humorous (The Muse and a Rose), iconoclastic (The Greek Defense), to the poignant (The Drawing, Two), the whimsical (The Transformation of Marmaduke), and the satirical (The Primary Candidate, The Zen of Deep Pit Latrines). There may be one or two that are about screw-ups. Some, I have been told, are challenging reads.

I am often asked who I write for. I don't know. I write what I feel and hope it is enjoyed by readers who like my style of writing.

I thank the members of the Florida Writers Association, Daytona Area Writers (Daytonaareawriters.com), and the City Island Fiction Writers for their help, support, and insightful critiques which have helped me immeasurably. Both are led by Veronica H. Hart who deserves special thanks, not least for putting up with me in manic and depressive writing modes, and the privilege of having her editing skills available at all times—well, most of the time.

Twisted Knickers—
A Bunch of Shorts (Stories)

Table of Contents

Inheritance 1

Release 7

The Greek Defense 9

Hopscotch 25

The Zen of Deep Pit Latrines 30

Hamburger, Anyone? 38

The Primary Candidate 43

Translocation 58

The Muse and a Rose 62

The Selfie Generation 72

Mud and Murder 83

Heidi and the Sikh 88

The Transformation of Marmaduke 94

The Drawing 100

The Riverboat..107

The Pickup 111

Two 114

I am Oliver, and I am a Cat...................................119

Inheritance

"Mrs. Wellday…" the detective began.

"Call me Belle. Everyone does."

"Be… Mrs. Wellday. First, let me say how sorry I am for your loss, but this is a death investigation and we need to understand what happened."

"It was that commercial where Lincoln's wife asks him if her dress makes her look fat." She pushed a family photo across the table. "He just put his stubby finger on me there and grinned."

"And…?"

"'You had hair on your head, and I had a shape. Once.' That's what I said to him. That's why I hate family photos. They should be banned, or taxed. I had shape! Look." Belle laced her hands in front of her belly and inhaled deeply. Then she pulled her housecoat around her body and sagged back on the chair like a wet feather mattress.

"And what did he say?" He glanced at the photograph.

"'Yeah, if you say so, and I had hair and shape too.' That's what he said. So I said, 'Bud, that beard? You call that hair?' He liked to be called Bud. 'It makes you look like a pervert.' And he gets all upset, see."

"You told him he was a pervert?"

Belle ignored her questioner. "So he says to me, 'Hey, just 'cause I spoke to that girl to find out where she was from, you call me a pervert?' That's what he said to me. So I told him like it was. 'You were hitting on a chick.' Then I say, 'So, Rooster Man, what did you say to her? Hey baby, look at my hairy shape?' 'Aw, shuddup,' he told me."

"And then?"

"I dunno. I poured myself another drink."

"You had been drinking?"

"You got something against that?"

"I'm just trying to get the picture."

"Yeah, well a great picture *he* made." Belle stabbed at the photograph with her podgy finger. "Look at him. His great belly sagging over his belt. He couldn't even reach his shoes to tie his laces. I bought him slip-ons at the flea market."

"So what happened?"

"He goes out like he always does."

"What did you do?"

"Watched *Law and Order*."

"What channel?"

"The one *Law and Order* was on."

"And then?"

"I fell asleep."

"Where?"

"Where? Jesus where do you think? On the damned sofa, that's where."

"You never went upstairs?"

"How could I go upstairs if I was asleep?"

"But you found him?"

"Yeah. In the bathroom. His brother died there too. Burst a blood vessel they said. He was straining 'cause he was constipated. Imagine. What a way to go, on the can."

"And he was where?"

"Where I told you, slumped on the can."

"Not the brother, Bud, your husband."

"Yeah. He was where you saw him. In the bath. That big hairy pervert. Right under the water he was. I didn't touch him. Just turned off the water because it was leaking all over the floor. That's why I went upstairs because of the water."

"You heard it running?"

"No, it was coming down the wall."

"And that's when you found him?"

"I thought he was still out."

"And you turned it off?"

"I told you that already."

"And his toe was like that when you found him, stuck in the faucet?"

"You think he put it there after he was dead?"

"No I meant—forget it."

"I told him to get rid of his belly, that's what I told him. He couldn't bend to sit up. His toe was stuck tight. I think he couldn't bend to turn the water off, so he stuck his toe in it, and then couldn't get it out. But it didn't stop the water."

"So he lay there until the water covered his face." The detective scribbled on a notepad. "You didn't hear him call or shout?"

"I told you, I was asleep."

"But you heard the water."

"I *saw* the water. Coming down the wall."

"You said you were asleep."

"After I woke up. Jesus, you men!"

"What woke you up?"

"I dunno. Must have been a commercial. They're so loud."

"What time was that?"

"Let's see, I needed to pee. *Law and Order* was over. So it must have been after ten."

"When did you see the water?"

"When I got up to pee. Hey, do you think it was the water made me want to pee?"

"You said you didn't hear it. Now, about his brother, Joshua. He died a few months ago, right?"

"April tenth. It was my birthday."

"And you found him."

"Like I said, he was on the can."

"He was sitting there when you found him?"

"Slumped against the wall."

"He had been constipated?"

"Always. Him and his bowel pills. And suppo—you know those things. I said he would blow up if he didn't get help. Did he listen? 'Course not. Men! You could hear his grunting all over the house."

"Police said they didn't find any laxatives in the bathroom."

"That's 'cause I flushed 'em down the can."

"You flushed them?"

"Well, he didn't need them no more, did he?"

"And this was after you found him?"

"What do you think?"

"There was another brother, wasn't there? Died suddenly?"

"No. My stepfather, Chuck. Died last year. Strangled."

"Strangled?"

"With his sheets. Tossing and turning in his sleep. Must have been a nightmare. They were all tight 'round his neck."

"His room was next to yours?"

"Right next door. Talk about snore. He made the room shake, tossing and turning. And pee? He was worse than me. Up and down all damn night. Prostrate or something."

"Prostate."

"Whatever."

"When did you find him?"

"When he stopped snoring. He went quiet. I waited a bit, I mean, I thought I could get some peace. Then he didn't snore again."

"And you didn't go back to sleep?"

"I was waiting for him to start snoring again. It was too quiet to sleep."

"Didn't..." The detective glanced at his notes. "Didn't Bud hear him?"

"Bud? He'd sleep through anything."

"Don't you have a sister?"

"Nah. She went too."

"Went?"

"Last summer. Dead. In the barn. There was this big fan I bought cheap for Bud to blow air through when he fixed cars. It'd been rewired, the fan. And she turned it on."

"In the barn."

"Yeah. It pulled her apron in. Then her. Chewed little bits off her face until there weren't nothing left. Bud said it had been wired backwards. Mistake."

"Who wired it?"

"Dunno. Musta been like that when Bud put it in. Can we finish this now?" Belle said.

"A couple more questions."

"Well, make it quick."

"So, there's no one left in the family now except you?"

"Hadn't thought of it like that. You're right."

"You have the whole place to yourself now."

"Yeah. Funny the way things work out."

"One more thing. How do you think Bud's toe, the stuck one, got Vaseline all over it?"

"Dunno. Maybe Bud put it on to help squeeze his toe in the faucet."

"But, didn't you say he was too fat to reach his toes?"

"Oh."

Release

The red light flashed ahead of him, waved slowly from side to side.

It could be any of them; the I.R.A., a British patrol, or the hated Northern Ireland B-Special police. It didn't matter. If he didn't stop they would shoot.

Brendan stamped on the brake. The car didn't slow. He pressed harder—harder, until he stood on the pedal. He grasped the steering wheel tighter. White knuckles crushed it to his chest.

The light flashed.

He sat up with a start, drenched in sweat. Light filtered through the bedroom window. Beside him on the nightstand his alarm blinked three-thirty. Bewildered, he took a moment to realize that there had been a power failure. He let go of the pillow he held tight against his chest and fell back. The ceiling faded and refocused as his panicked heart sought a calmer rhythm.

Could he ever escape? Surely one day their aim would steady. One day he would be theirs. He fumbled for the cigarettes by his bedside. There were none. His hand hit the empty glass. Cigarettes and the sweet smell of Scotch, his night-time companions.

Sleep came slowly. It was never hard to wake; just terrifying.

He stumbled to the bathroom to rinse the sour taste of bile from his mouth. Red rimmed eyes stared from the mirror, their whites seared with spidery lines from staring at the light night after night.

More details of the dream returned. The long winding road, silent and empty at the midnight hour. He raced through the dark, knowing the border closed at two a.m. Tires squealed on the corners, the back of the car twitching and sliding as it fought to break away. He was aware of the ditches lining the road; ditches that could hold a Saracen armored car, or a man under a soft brimmed cap, his hand poised over a plunger and its promise of oblivion blowing metal and limbs skyward—a message from the enemy.

One night, he knew, he would not awake in time. He would not stop. And he would feel again the hail of bullets rake his car, and the searing pain as his ear was ripped from his skull by flying glass, and watch the body fly in the air, as it had done so many years ago when his car hit the light and the man who held it. Only he knew this time they would shoot more than his ear.

How much longer could he last? How many more dreams could he endure? Perhaps–just perhaps—he could thwart their efforts. Deny them the satisfaction of revenge. Kill the dream. Kill it dead.

He returned to his bed. Before he lay back, he pulled the 9mm from his bedside drawer. He fingered the side of his head, where his ear had been. There would be nothing in the way of a clean shot.

He raised his gun.

The Greek Defense

Zeus and unlicensed supplements.

With acknowledgements to Homer and a bunch of Greek

and Roman historians.

The Odyssey is the sexist story of Odysseus's journey home to Greece from Troy at the end of the Trojan War, 1194–1184 BC. This King of Ithaca, (not the one in upstate New York,) left his faithful wife Penelope as a single mom twenty years earlier to help his buddy King Menelaus get his wife, Helen, back.

Helen's cause launched an armada of 1000 ships, exhausting the Greek supply of champagne, and creating schools of tipsy fish.

There are two parts to this story. The Trojan War, related in the Iliad, and the return of Odysseus to Ithaca told in the Odyssey. Both are written as classical stories of reverence and praise. I can now provide a corrected interpretation of his return.

Odysseus spent ten years playing the horses in Troy before he claimed a winning ticket, razed the city in his exuberance, and then spent nine years on a journey home which should have taken three weeks. Had Ithaca and Troy been in upstate New York we might have given him the benefit of the doubt. However, in true Greek heroic fashion he blamed the Gods, "The Gods made me do it," while being comforted on his journey home by the odd divine mistress or two.

On closer inspection it appears Odysseus was no saint. He was a draft dodger, a philanderer, and a chronic shipwreck survivor. There is also a rumor that he didn't taste good, as he survived when all the rest of his men either drowned, or were eaten. He killed others as an easy cure for problems. And he probably lied to his wife when he got home, unless she bought the God Defense.

This story started Greek history, complicated by "The Gods," which kings, queens, and Greek heroes claim as relatives, because this makes them, and their ancestors look good. The gods can also be blamed by the Greeks for every sexual indiscretion, thus sparing them the embarrassment suffered by present day politicians. It appears that royalty, political leaders and celebrities were, as today, the god's chief clients.

Odysseus was the hero created by Homer, a blind poet and wandering minstrel. Homer would have written it down at the time but he had not yet been invented. Neither had Greek writing. Anyway, he couldn't see.

Let him sing to you the first verse of exactly what happened.

Sing about Odysseus, and his girls of course.
Four and twenty soldiers hidden in a horse.
When the horse was opened, the soldiers, so they say,
Murdered all the Trojan men, and took their girls away (for play) (foreplay) whatever.

The Greeks remedied the voice problem 400 years later by stealing Sumerian or Phoenician letters and calling it the Greek alphabet. Then they learned to write, invented

Homer, and left out the singing.

In the classic version, Odysseus returned to Ithaca (not in upstate New York), to find a bunch of lusting suitors stalking his queen. With the assistance of the gods, his son, and a friend, Odysseus killed them all and reclaimed his kingdom. The moral of the story is said to show that virtue wins over deception.

Before we look at his real reluctant homecoming, perhaps we should examine why he went in the first place.

The Trojan War

This period of history was started, as were so many, by a dispute over a woman, Helen, daughter of Zeus, the King of the Gods which assured her place in history. She can thus take her place beside other famous women, Eve, Cleopatra, Mrs. Borgia, Joan of Arc, Pocahontas, Annie Oakley, and an early morning drunk, Bloody Mary, who invented the barbecue (see *The Muse and a Rose*).

Contrary to popular belief that she was a hypnotic beauty (per Aphrodite, another deity), Helen was a chronic abductee, a child bride, an underage teenage mom long before she wasted all the champagne, and subsequently a serial killer. And along the way she had a few lovers.

Of course, she could always say, "The Gods made me do it," and probably did.

Theseus, as son of a god (not the same as SOB), thought he should have a divine wife. So he abducted Helen when she was either seven or ten years old, which makes him a pedophile. He would not have been allowed within a stadia or two of Plato's academy once it existed. They also had a daughter, Iphigenia, which put Helen of childbearing age and possibly made Theseus a statutory rapist. Or Helen may have been very precocious.

Helen's brothers Castor and Pollux rescued her, and

11

took her back to Sparta. Perhaps she was not as pure as suggested. She has been described as a young princess wrestling naked in the palestra, an ancient Greek wrestling school. Quite an image. Sextus Propertius imagines Helen "on the sands of Eurotas, with naked breasts she carried weapons, they say, and did not blush with her divine brothers there." How he got into the act is uncertain as he is Roman and they had not yet been invented.

Shortly after her return home, King Tyndareus decided that it was time for her to marry, give her and the baby a name—daughter of Zeus, Top God, wasn't enough apparently—and get her off his hands. Besieged by powerful suitors (forty-five in number, including Odysseus), whichever one Tyndareus might choose, he could anger the others. Bummer, or equivalent ancient Greek expression.

Odysseus didn't think he had much chance, so he promised to solve the problem, if Tyndareus would help him court Penelope. Helen's dad made a political pact after Odysseus advised him to have all the suitors take an oath during the primaries to accept the choice for Helen on the first ballot, and promise to support that chosen person whenever needed. The suitors agreed, (for the time being), and Tyndareus chose Menelaus.

Odysseus won Penelope.

***

For a while, Helen and Menelaus lived happily. They had a couple of kids, and Menelaus became king of Sparta, just normal routine life. But in the wings, with the help of the gods, lurked Paris, a prince of Troy. He traveled to Sparta on the advice of Aphrodite, another scheming little goddess.

To put this in divine perspective, Eris, the goddess of strife, gave the goddesses Athena, Hera, and Aphrodite, a golden apple—the Apple of Discord— to be given to the fairest of them, which sent them all into a tizzy. Zeus, Top

God, sent the bunch to see Paris, to judge them.

They first bathed in the spring of Ida, then paraded naked in front of him, either to help their chances of winning, or because Paris asked them to. Even taking his time, Paris couldn't make up his mind, so the chilly Goddesses tried to bribe him. Athena said she would make him a great warrior; Hera would give him political power; but Aphrodite, the crafty one, knew her way around a loin or two and offered him the love of the most beautiful woman in the world. No contest.

Paris awarded Aphrodite the apple in exchange for Aphy giving Helen a makeover and getting her to fall for him with the help of Cupid, the chubby little cherub with a bow and arrow. Paris then abducted her to Troy (not in upstate New York).

Well, maybe she went of her own accord, but as she *was* married to Menelaus at the time it seems more diplomatic to say abducted—for the second time.

When Menelaus returned home and discovered Helen gone, he called on the leaders of Greece who had sworn to support him if necessary. Odysseus was now married and a dad. Being so far from the Canadian border he instead feigned madness to escape the draft, but his ruse was tumbled, and off he went.

Their arrival at Troy marked the beginning of the Trojan War.

It seemed to be a Greek specialty to abduct women. Europa was abducted from Phoenicia; Hesione, taken by Heracles; Jason grabbed Medea from Colchis; and Io was snatched from Mycenae. I don't know who any of these people were, and I doubt you do either. All that counts is that the Greeks had an abduction standard which they had to live up to. Blame it on the gods. Paris figured he could steal a wife from Greece with no problem; the others got away with it.

He hadn't figured on Menelaus or their Republican style oath.

During the war, Helen, true to form, played each side against the other. At times she fingered the Greek leaders to the Trojans. At other times she let them risk figuring it out themselves.

Eventually, Helen, tired of Paris, decided he had weaknesses, and hedged her bet (bed) with his brother Hector. When they both copped it in battle, she took up with their younger brother, Deiphobus, to keep it in the family, but he was only temporary. When the Greeks climbed off their high horse, she hid her new husband's sword and let Menelaus and Odysseus deal with him.

Menelaus finally found her, but when he raised his sword to kill her, she let her robe fall. At the sight of her—beauty—he dropped it, or raised it, depending what you were thinking of. Then Helen and Menelaus set sail for Sparta. Possibly he abducted her.

The Greeks acted like a rowdy, well a rowdier, soccer crowd, killed pretty near everyone and desecrated the temples. People were okay; temples were a definite no-no.

After he helped kill all the Trojans, Odysseus hoped to go home, but, by ruining the temples, he pissed off Poseidon, later to be known as Neptune. The God decided most of the Greeks would never see their homeland again. Even Oddy's very close 'friend' and supporter, the goddess Athena, felt abused

So where did these gods come from? And where did they disappear to? That's the point of creation stories. These questions have been, until now, confused by historians.

Zeus was a third generation god after the initial Chaos and the first divine generation, followed by the Titans. Zeus took over by beating the Titans and setting himself up as Top God on Mount Olympus.

He was Top God of a dozen Great Greek Gods, as

carved on a frieze (freeze?) in the Parthenon, and modelled as statues in the British Museum after a couple of thousand years, wearing little or no clothing

In a modern classical education, all Great Greeks come in threes— three Great Greek Historians, three Great Greek Playwrights, three Great Greek Philosophers. Renowned for his sexual appetite, Zeus fathered children with dozen of goddesses and mortals producing many more than three Greek Gods.

The lives of the Greek billionaire upper classes were based, much like today, on priests, shamans, sorcerers, and diviners, nowadays called Financial Advisors and Lawyers. These remarkable persons had visions, saw wondrous things, prophesied, told fortunes, painted incredible figures, and could feed their supplicants enough *soma* to get them in a receptive state for whatever the wishes of the gods, or the shaman wanted.

Torn between powerful goddesses, and getting what they wanted from their own women 'friends,' or the ones they lusted for, their society was a recipe for a potpourri of psychic rulers and believing congregations. Because the shamans couldn't write, and the populace couldn't read, it was easy to keep secrets.

We should define "gods," as opposed to "God"— otherworldly critters having supernatural powers, with whom humans could mess around, and blame for everything.

"The concept of a god" is still in our language, and if reality is defined by language, as some believe, then the gods are still around. Provided language names them, they exist. Keep looking over your shoulder. Possibly you may need the Greek Defense in court one day.

It was one thing to believe in gods who pleased themselves, but how did they get to influence, politics, wars, and liaisons? This happened when shrines were built, and young ladies installed to care for oracles. They interpreted the god's wishes.

The ladies were really shamans who had visions, magical experiences, and could "help" their clients to see strange things and believe even stranger things. How?

Once again, as later in Britain, it was due to diet, in this case unlicensed supplements.

Evidence for the use of cannabis, opioids, magic mushrooms, and other mind altering drugs, has been found in periods of human history, before Timothy Leary, from 60,000 to 40,000 years BC. The Greeks were a drop in Poseidon's ocean. Chew enough, swallow enough, or smoke enough, and man, can you imagine gods.

And their wine differed from ours. It was laced with everything that couldn't be chewed or smoked. So generous religious libations could do a number on shamans and clients alike.

Blame the gods for everything? Did they ever. Thanks to the masterful invention of Zeus and his sexual appetite, they produced a god to cover every contingency.

When the status of Greek gods began to wane, the Romans took over, Romanized them, and changed their names. With the rise of Christianity, these pagan gods were phased out and replaced by saints. Despite our legal ability to hold various personal religious beliefs, 'the saints made me do it' is a more difficult defense.

In 1639, a revisionist Italian historian, Monteverdi, with the help of his buddy Giacomo Badaoro, otherwise known as a librettist, wrote his own version of Greek history with *Il Ritorno d'Ulisse in Patria*, *The Return of Ulysses to his Homeland,* an interminable Italian opera in a prologue and five acts (later revised to a similarly interminable three) which they first staged in Venice.

Up to the Trojan War the gods had favored the

Greeks, probably because the Trojans didn't have any decent ones of their own. This was about to change.

The Journey Home

Once he left Troy, storms drove Odysseus's ships off course. They visited the Lotus-Eaters, and were then captured by the cyclops, Polyphemus, while visiting his island, who ate some of his men. Homer had a thing about eating people later celebrated in song.

Odysseus fed Polyphemus a whole barrel of wine and, once drunk, blinded him with a flaming stake. Nice. Odysseus and his crew then, being brave warriors, hid underneath sheep, escaped from the island, but met more cannibals, the giant Laestrygonians. Odysseus's ship was the only one to escape. Only those on his ship survived. The rest were eaten.

He sailed on and visited the witch-goddess Circe. She turned half of his men into swine after feeding them laced cheese and wine. And let them eat anything.

Hermes, another God, warned Odysseus about Circe and gave Odysseus a drug called *moly*, probably garlic. Circe, fell in love with him, despite his garlic breath, and released his men. The ones who hadn't yet been eaten.

After a year his restless men (there was only one Circe, and she was spoken for) complained that it was time to go home. She advised them on the remaining stages of the journey. They nipped past the Sirens, and sailed between the six-headed monster Scylla and the whirlpool Charybdis, but not before Scylla dragged the boat toward her and ate six more men.

Odysseus must have been close to running out of men, or Homer's math was rough.

They landed on the island of Thrinacia. There, Odysseus's men ignored the warnings of Circe and hunted the sacred cattle of the sun god Helios, and probably ate them. Helios whined to Zeus and blackmailed the Top God to punish Odysseus' men. He threatened to shine the sun into the Underworld, cause local climate change, and upset nature. So Zeus arranged a shipwreck during a thunderstorm. They all drowned except Odysseus. None were left to be eaten.

He was washed ashore on an island where Calypso compelled him to remain as her lover for seven years. Homer writes that Calypso was "a nymph, immortal and most beautiful, who craved Odysseus for her own." We grieve for him. Homer, of course, had never seen her, since she was in fact a myth, and Homer, being blind, couldn't appreciate her beauty. Bummer.

One day, with Poseidon away in distant Ethiopia, the goddess Athena, Odysseus' protector, petitioned Zeus and the other gods to rescue Odysseus from Calypso. Homer doesn't make clear if Odysseus really begged the gods to allow him to escape, or that is Athena's jealous version of the story. Anyway, Calypso had worn him out, and Homer claimed he pined for home. So, he finally escaped, was shipwrecked again, and befriended by the Phaeacians.

When he arrived at wherever the Phaeacians lived, Nausicaa, a nubile princess, was playing volley-ball on the beach with her handmaidens.

Athena had disguised Odysseus as a beggar, looking like a refugee from series one of Survivor, but that didn't take much magic after being on the road for nine years, so, hiding his embarrassing parts behind an olive branch, he staggered into the bunch of young women. A wardrobe malfunction sent the handmaidens away screaming or giggling, but not Nausicaa.

"It must be quite difficult to listen to a naked man and take him seriously," but Nausicaa was nothing if not modern. The teenage princess, with her own hormonal pressures, took him home to meet mummy and daddy. After telling them his sob story, the Phaeacians, led by daddy, King Alcinous, agreed to help Odysseus get home quickly—and away from his daughter.

They dropped him off at a hidden harbor in Ithaca while he was fast asleep.

Homecoming

Odysseus returned to a chubbier wife. He may have had a pot himself. His muscles had weakened from high living with all his girlfriends and fathering so many kids (more about that later). She had OCD, weaving, unraveling, weaving, unraveling. For twenty years.

He told her that the Gods made him do it, and all his men were eaten, so they couldn't contradict him.

Penelope had set up a test for the suitors to see who could string Odysseus' bow. None of the suitors were able to. It was never said why he went to war leaving his weapon behind. Penelope explained in her long interview with the disguised hero that whoever could string the bow of Apollo, Odysseus's rigid bow, and shoot an arrow through twelve rings, or axe shafts, depending on whose Homeric version you believe, may have her hand, and presumably the rest of her body.

Odysseus' identity was rumbled by the housekeeper as she washed his feet and discovered an old scar Odysseus received during a boar hunt. Odysseus swore her to secrecy, threatening to kill her if she told anyone. Typical.

"'Ecco l'arco Ulysse'—behold the bow of Ulysses," Penelope cried as the last suitor raised his bow, before the setting sun "rang in the curfew" on their pitiful attempts. Well that's what they sang in the opera, so who am I to judge? That was in Italian, because Greek is harder to read and sing. If she really had been Greek she would have said Ασημένιο Τόξο και Βέλος, or, 'Behold the silver bow,' something like that.

Now Odysseus didn't understand Italian because Romans hadn't been invented yet, so he didn't know what the hell she was singing. Also his language skills were probably a bit rusty having wandered in foreign lands for so long, and Troy was in Hissalik, Turkey, where they didn't speak Italian, which hadn't been invented.

Oh, what the hell. He picked up the bow. Damn. It was much stiffer than he expected. Must be the years it had sat idle. But he felt it was his duty to rescue his wife, changed though she may be from those suitors drooling after her, and her—his, riches, even if their marriage had been somewhat barren. Well except for Telemarcus, but he was conceived in the throes of youthful passion.

After the suitors had given up, the disguised Odysseus entered stage left, bent the bow, shot the arrow, and won the contest. Then he slaughtered the suitors, and told the serving women who slept with the suitors to clean up the mess of corpses—then had those women hanged. Nice.

He told his son, Telemachus, that he would replenish his stocks by raiding nearby islands, adding plunderer to his resume. Odysseus had now revealed himself in all his glory (with a little makeover by Athena); yet Penelope could not believe that her husband had really returned—she feared that it was perhaps some god in disguise. Still skeptical, she wasn't above testing him in bed, it is said by him trying to move the bed, which may be interpreted as how boisterous he still was!

A "gasping Penelope" finally accepted that he truly was her husband—that's what Homer wrote!—a moment that highlighted their *homophrosýnē*. You can look it up. It only means like-mindedness.

Many, many, years later, a son of his with the witch Circe, Telegonus, had grown up. The boy wanted to meet his long lost father, filed a paternity suit, and set out to sea to find him. But when he landed on Ithaca, hungry and alone, he killed some sheep for food. Old King Odysseus thought he was a pirate, and armed with spears popped down to the shore to chase him away.

Like father, like son. The macho pair fought not knowing who the other was. Daddy lost, his chest run through by a spear tipped with the poison sting of a ray. This fulfilled the prophecy that his death would come from the sea, but I forget who made it.

The story's not quite over. Telegonus took Penelope and Telemachus to Circe's island, where mummy made them immortal. The two sons then married each other's mothers. Kinky.

So we had a happy kind of incestuous ending.

***

Some intellectual historians consider that Homer's story is a myth about a man in a midlife crisis, whose wife Penelope suffered from the cabbage syndrome from sitting at home weaving all day, and never getting out. Some, probably jealous, report him fathering a bunch of brats which Monteverdi and his buddy Giacomo Badaoro ignored, including three with Circe and two with Calypso, but I did find a daughter and fifteen boys before I lost count.

The Romans later traced their origin to Aeneas, one of the Trojan survivors. He was said to have led the survivors to modern-day Italy and invented Monteverdi. They believed Odysseus, who they renamed Ulisse, was a complete villain. Virgil made this point in his famous line *"timeo Danaos et dona ferentes,* I fear Greeks, even those bearing gifts."

If there is one fact that guarantees that this story is a myth, it is Penelope's name. In Greek, the meaning is *with a web over her face,* related to her weaving. But she had her name before she married or started to mislead the suitors by weaving. Go figure.

The Romans, who would have you believe Odysseus was a villain, and had a quirky sense of humor, suggested her name was derived from Greek, *penelops*, a breed of duck.

One good thing emerged from telling these incredibly long and involved mythological stories. Once they had swiped the Phoenician alphabet and taught themselves to write, the Greeks had lots of material to practice with.

Homer started the celebrity cult, setting the standard for spin, and getting Oddy off to a good start. Wonder what Homer would make of today's developments?

This updated expose of ancient Greece tells how little has changed in a couple of millennia, showing how unimaginative biographers can be. They still write only about personalities, heroes, nymphs, or sirens, and their amoral behavior gets a pass because of their mass appeal—that's who we want to be, and not get caught. Privilege and macho redneckism are unchanged.

Homer's view of the masculine paranoia over women shows how men praised their beauty, feared their power over men, or alternatively, were ashamed of their own male weakness. Sound familiar? The Greeks got away with putting their nymphs and sirens on pedestals, yet rigidly controlling them. That last bit has gone by the wayside.

C'est la vie.

I found the Bardic version of the story on which this myth is based. The music has been lost.

> Sing about Odysseus, and his girls of course.
> Four and twenty soldiers, hidden in a horse.
> When the horse was opened, the soldiers, so they say,
> Murdered all the Trojan men, and took their girls
> away. (for play) (foreplay) whatever.

> Penelope in Ithaca, weaved her life away.

Three bad suitors waited, with her to have "their
way."
Then her man returnéd. She proved his worth in bed,
He lifted up his trusty bow, and shot the suitors dead.

He was gray and older, and she was somewhat tubby.
But she was still his loving wife, and he was still her
hubby.
Argus recognized him, his faithful dog, 'tis said,
Smiled at him and gave his paw—and then rolled
over dead.

Returned within his family, he swore to stay at home.
That lasted twenty minutes, before the urge to roam.
Homer didn't write this, his book was clearly done,
He'd started Greece's history, but Oddy'd had the
fun.

Hopscotch

A game played throughout the world since recorded history.

It is said that one sees what one expects to see.

Bernard's wife had just left the Monday early-morning service at The Drive-by Church of Our Ladies of the Perpetual Blue Rinse, when Collins, an intellectually challenged adult waif she had taken under her bosom, it being bigger than her wing, decided to carry out her request and shoot her husband. She had told Collins his route and time to travel to work. She decided to lurk near Collins once his decision had been made, to encourage him and witness that he did in fact do it. She would thus have a patsy if questioned, or seen at the scene of the crime.

That morning, as Karma would have it, while she was yet driving by the early morning service, her husband, Bernard, had called an associate for a lift to work because his car battery had yielded its electrical soul to the afterlife.

Collins recognized the car but had insufficient time to mentally process that it was not indeed Bernard's car. Thus as the target and said associate drove by, Collins drew out a vintage Korean War revolver provided by Bernard's wife, and fired at the driver to send him to join the dead battery, before first asking to see his ID, and establish if he was indeed Bernard.

Bernard, in the passenger seat, recognized the shooter, and saw the familiar figure of his wife hovering in the background.

"Take this," Collins cried, handing Mrs. Bernard the revolver. Then he sprinted off down the road with minimal procrastination.

Mrs. Bernard put the revolver in her purse then without looking at the car, turned her back on the scene and, like Collins, boogied out of there.

Collins had shot the wrong man. Neither knew this, since in fear of being rumbled, they had, as mentioned, fled.

The police, swiftly for that area, particularly on a Monday—although come to think of it, Monday being a good day for murder, they may have deployed more men to earn overtime and thus win the approval of the Union—sealed the roads, questioned anyone they could apprehend, and retired with their bounty of passing souls to the local precinct. Thus it was that Bernard, astonished though he appeared to be, was able to recognize Mrs. Bernard and Collins in a hastily called line-up at the local nick without them knowing he was indeed alive.

The legal brains hastily summoned, dripping, from the pool of public defenders, dived into a chilling argument, which served to wake them up, about the propriety of relying on a close relative to finger the innocent protesting pair when he might well be considered to be biased in his judgment due to a disputed insurance claim.

It appears Mrs. Bernard had filed for her husband's death prematurely before Collins had done the deed, Collins being prone to procrastinate when contemplating any move requiring a decision. This she argued had not happened, and if it had happened, the insurance claim was post-dated, or she didn't know about it, whichever came first.

His wife claimed she had nothing to do with the driver's death, following her belief that to lie, lie, lie, was the best defense, and anyway she had made a valiant attempt to stop Collins on her arrival after being blessed at the drive-by service.

"So, you were there?" she was asked by the law, pulsing in the blue light of justice coming through the window from a police car parked outside.

"What do you mean?"

"You said you tried to stop Collins from shooting."

"Why, do you think it was him?"

"Did you try to stop him?"

"I meant I prayed he would never harm my husband."

"So you are saying," the officer said, "that you had nothing to do..." Before he could finish, Mrs. Barnard chimed in.

"I had nothing to do with shooting my husband."

"Your husband? Shooting? Quite."

"Collins must have planned it for weeks."

"Shooting your husband?"

"Who do you think? Anyway, it was Bernard's fault for being there in the wrong place at the wrong time."

"You deny being dead?" the Officer asked Bernard after his wife denied killing him, but was obviously convinced he was dead.

"I leave that up to you," he replied.

"I must ask for the record."

"In that case, I am alive."

The detective in charge, wiser and sharper than either Collins or Mrs. Bernard, realized in a Eureka moment, after the briefest delay, that Mrs. Bernard should not have thought she knew the identity of the victim unless she was in some way connected to the incident. And of course, she had been caught in the dragnet that rounded up so many innocent people.

When asked of his role in the conspiracy to deprive a man of his life, Collins took some time to answer, he being prone to procrastinate due to processing the request. He then equally vehemently denied killing Barnard. "Anyhow," he said. "Where would I get bullets for an old revolver like that?"

"Like what?"

"Like the one that killed Bernard."

"Where is it now?"

"I don't know. I gave it back to Mrs. Bernard."

It had been several weeks earlier that Bernard realized his wife was indulging herself in an affair with his close associate. After hours of meditation on his navel, when he was occasionally able to glimpse it, he considered what she planned for the immediate future. He did of course, harbor some transient fears for his own safety. Thus he intended to thwart whatever plans his wife might have if he could divine them. In lieu of that, he must preempt them, or in familiar current jargon, be proactive.

At first, he came to no firm conclusions on how to proceed so he decided to stir the pot by cultivating his associate's friendship. The proof that he was on the right track came when the insurance company contacted him about his premature death, and assured him, that had he indeed met with an accidental or violent end, they would honor their commitment to pay him double.

In passing, Barnard mentioned to his wife that he had read that Monday appeared to be the day when most murders occurred, and with police stretched to their limit the odds of being apprehended were thusly less. And he took out his vintage revolver and cleaned it in her presence.

Still unaware of her husband's continued sojourn in the land of the living, and now complicating her role by further denouncing Collins, Mrs. Bernard was remanded to the cells to await arraignment for charges she could not comprehend.

Collins, who thought being accused of anything by the police was par for the course, accepted the overnight accommodation without protest at the time, he being prone to procrastinate.

Later that evening, Bernard took the opportunity to call his associate's wife and commiserate with her on their mutual spousal difficulties, and ask if she needed help filing her own insurance claim as he had recently familiarized himself with the procedure. She invited him over.

He picked up the bottle of Cabernet he had bought several days before, to help him over his shock at his wife's intended duplicity, and to help his associate's wife over her husband's death, and whistling, drove to the house of his former associate in a car with a spontaneously resurrected battery.

She welcomed him wearing little more than a big smile.

They looked forward to seeing the guilty ones in court.

The Zen of Deep Pit Latrines

An evening of profound intellectualism.

I expected to cover a Harley motorcycle event; instead I had been drafted to cover a theatrical production. "Have to support the arts," the editor said, and he instructed me, instructed no less, to wear suit and tie.

Now I had just witnessed an evening of performance art where a semi-naked man climbed a tree as a monkey, then accompanied by grunts and guttural noises, he evolved during a remarkably convoluted production accompanied by various instruments from cymbals to skin drums and flutes, into a fully clothed sentient being, presumably on a par with the playwright-director. It was a pity that at some stage he lost his tail as that provided the only light relief, particularly when it lodged in a fork in the tree and the primitive monkey taught us that they expressed frustration in the same way as us with "f*ck."

I would be lying if I told you I understood the play, or the rest of the evening, but I had been *instructed* again to show that our backwater crossroads junction was *up there* with the sharpest intellects in the county.

My coverage included the post production reception and a promise of a personal introduction to the playwright, which was expected to include one handshake and thirty seconds of shared staccato phonemes that substituted for a conversation.

Standing invisible at the edge of the room, I slipped into people-watching mode outside the event horizon of this body of the self-appointed intellectual elite. I skirted the edge of their world, watching the swirls and eddies of what passed for polite discourse, as groups formed, heads nodding, smiled, and dispersed to possibly more interesting or noticeable guests. Those with the loudest voices or laughs attracted the most body traffic which hovered politely for the shortest times.

Perhaps I should have tried to flaunt a sense of class by wearing no socks and drinking beer from the bottle. Except, I saw no beer.

As if at a Halloween party, the guests wore apparel from Bohemian to the first night on Broadway, circa 1930. Torn jeans and off the shoulder blouses, one shoulder, to Salvation Army dresses vying with Dior and Halston. An excess of dresses in slimming black may have been because they were little and revealed much.

I had just grabbed a miniscule flute of a bubbly liquid when buttonholed, a polite way of saying pinned to the wall, by the organizer. Undressed in a little black nothing.

"It's Sydney," she said. "With a Z and a terminal E."

"Zydneye."

I had just sat through a terminal evening.

Another flute of cheap bubbly swept from a waiter's hand into mine as he passed. He may have been a guest, but I took it anyway. The evening was having a strange effect on me.

Obviously we had not yet finally emerged from this experience of Performance Art. She gushed to me about the depth of the experiential permissiveness that successfully undermined the traditional artificiality of commercialism and exposed the raw essence of the emotional trauma suffered by the true artist.

I agreed, what else could I do? I write. I get paid. I'm the enemy; a commercial writer for fun and profit. About to contradict her, my drink disappeared in one gulp. My hand reached for another. My brain cells needed lubricating.

She was about to expand on the angst induced in the audience—I believe that is what she attempted to tell me—when I decided to join the fray. The effect of her affect—or the champagne.

"Indeed," I said. "I stand in awe of your sensitivity in the face of the collective disparity between an audience which lacks discrimination and the cries of the misunderstood artist striving to bridge the gulf of ignorance. That, I know, you see."

"You noticed," she said.

"Excreta Tauris intelligentsia perplexit," I said, scrambling declension, or was it conjugation, feeling sure she wouldn't understand whether the genital, I mean genitive, ending of a bull should be –is, or –i. Latin gave me up in the sixth grade. Actually, that's when I started, but existentially, they amount to the same thing. But of one thing I was sure— bullshit always perplexes the intelligent.

"It is so gratifying to meet someone, at last, in this commercial backwater, with your understanding," she said.

"Thank you."

The reception was held in Le, or perhaps La Galleria. A sparse arrangement of art work, the occasional statue, notable bust or two (marble or bronze, outnumbered by the flesh), not being an art critic, none of which, or whom, I recognized.

A particularly offensive picture of a bird snatching a butterfly from a group of garish flowers caught my eye as it roamed round the room independent of my brain. My mouth seized on it, also independent of my brain. I stood as if in a park listening to a mime as my voice took over.

"The metaphor of death amidst beauty is a universal theme," I heard myself say, "challenging the psyche to choose, bird or butterfly. Ripping its squirming body from the beauty of the flower, where it hungers for the unity of existence. While the flower weeps it knows not for what."

"My God," she said.

"It represents a deep universal sadness which mirrors the theme of the play. Who eventually triumphs in such a contest? Does the flower feel guilt for attracting the butterfly to its death? Or does the butterfly welcome death?"

She smiled and emptied her glass into her maw.

"In the words of the Punjabi poet, Ghalib," I said. "'Love knows no difference between life and death.'"

I had to be careful I didn't bull-shit myself. It was obvious she wouldn't recognize *excreta tauris*, even if she stepped in it.

"This is so true," she said.

"Your enlightened comment indicates an understanding as expressed in the *bayt-ul-khala,*" I said. "When Shitsid the Elder, you may remember, toyed with the intensity of self destruction in the face of the depth to which one could fall into disgust."

She took my face in her hands, hampered somewhat by the plastic wine-glass, if I might be excused for calling it that, still clasped between the fingers of her right hand, and gazed deep into my eyes, breathing cheap Champagne fumes. "Can I quote you?"

She staggered slightly as someone grasped her arm. "You must meet the author," the newcomer wheezed through a cloud of smoke from her thin cheroot clasped inelegantly in a holder, imitating a 1920's flapper, thus saving me from explaining the workings of a *bayt-ul-khala,* an Urdu deep pit latrine. Quite disgusting if you fall in. Then the newcomer moved on. Her lips still moving.

"I believe opera alone obviates the necessity to stretch one's understanding as the temporal effects of music overwhelm the natural tendency for the emotions to lag behind," I said, before Zydneye, with a Z and a terminal E, could continue. "Although it can be due to the uncomfortable seats."

She looked at me sharply. Then I think she thought she got the joke and smiled; a quirky smile that came and went quickly several times before deciding to stay.

"You can be so deep," she said. "I thought I grasped the Eastern dichotomy relating to the western existential experience, until I met you."

She had me there, so I plunged on. "Had Freud not so underestimated the power of sang, we would not have been faced with mistranslations of Sartre's idiomatic French."

"Sang?" she said.

"Sorry, professional idiom." I did not go on to explain sangfroid. "Such an experience sends intellectual chills deep into the imperturbability of the emotional seat of reason."

Her smile was fading. As was my ability to understand myself. She appeared to be about to excuse herself to meet the author where they could rub psyches together to generate sparks of mutual admiration, when she hesitated.

"Emotions are the key to the soul's depth, as we heard tonight," she said.

"I was impressed by the idiomatic use of the analogy to an inverted tautology reminiscent of the argument Camus might have used had he met Aristotle. Don't you agree?"

She nodded while smiling, weakly.

I thought my reasoned argument, in the Aristotelian sense, had created an escape route from more self-anointed literati whose pomposity trumps talent or achievement. Was I joining that enlightened group? I grabbed another flute.

Then the author came into earshot. There should have been a finger on the trigger.

"Of course we should be supported by the state, darling," he said. "We are the ones that preserve what few works of intellect are left for posterity. It is so crass that we should be required to write commercial shite to make a living."

Where had he learned that word? Perhaps he felt it represented a higher form of emotional excretion.

I thought to tell him he could wait on tables, or serve behind a bar, but I doubted he would see the honesty in such an approach. Or like the work.

As this evening seemed to revolve about the spreading of b.s., instead I told him that I applauded those who had the courage to embrace intellectual coprolites, without explaining that it meant fossilized excrement—hard pieces of literary gobshite, as Joyce might say.

The author paused to stare deeply into my eyes with an unfocused gaze. "I believe we truly understand each other," he said. He would have slapped me on the back, but fortunately a glass in each hand precluded that.

"Shakespeare wrote for the commercial theatre, and Dickens earned his living writing," I offered. "How did they get away with it?"

"Don't mention Shakespeare, that charlatan. He filched all his plots and had underemployed courtiers to do most of the writing. You tell me! How do you suppose a country bumpkin knew so much about the royal courts and Italy?"

About to say National Geographic, he cut me off.

"And Dickens. He wrote serials for the newspaper. Serials! Like those terrible films they made us sit through on Saturday mornings as kids. A few cents for a seat and a cup of soda. The screen was our babysitter."

"How do you account for their fame?"

"Oh, I don't think either of them was ever *really* famous as a writer, well, not until Hollywood made their meager efforts into film noire using famous actors, darling— from the stage."

Film noire? Had he forgotten Elizabeth Taylor and Richard Burton, and sixty-nine ways of displaying her overloaded bra in Cleopatra? In full vibrant color. Perhaps he was too young.

Even I could see his grasp of literary criticism and intellectual ability was strictly bounded by a profound wall of ignorance.

I have yet to rationalize the difference between literary and commercial writers. The glorious Bard was commercial. So too Chuck Dickens. Sir Walter Scott wrote to pay off debts. Yet the appellation of literary connotes a higher standing in the writing world – or does it? Are literary writers given the accolade because their writing is less easily understood? Or because they can use words like shite instead of shit?

Blame it on Pavlov. I have been conditioned. If I have not been 'found' how can I ever be literary? Better settle for commercial, even though it hasn't paid too many bills so far.

I had reached the limit of my ability, or desire, to maintain the b.s. I was not sure about Zydneye, Z, terminal E, although she appeared ready for my departure.

I was also running out of long words.

"As *bahut bahut shukriya*, said," I said, using what little Urdu I remembered to say 'thank you very much.' Did I mention I spent part of my childhood in the Punjab? My Ayah taught me expressions in Urdu, some of which would have shocked my parents, had they known.

"Mai aap se mohabbat karta hun."

She stared, deeply moved, as I bent to kiss her hand, not knowing I had just told her, unable to think of anything else to say, that I loved her.

I took my leave fully expecting my written piece could well be my last, and hopefully rid me of pretentious gobbledygook. I set off to the nearest bar for a proper drink.

I went back several nights later for several more.

My efforts at obfuscatory b.s. had not had the desired effect. I have been asked to address the Zydneye, Z terminal E, Artistic Collective about how the deep eastern influence on the expression of western feelings forces the development of our intrapersonal striving for truth.

Perhaps I could lecture on The Zen of Deep Pit Latrines?

In fact, there might be a literary book in it!

Hamburger, Anyone?

One does not expect to crack a tooth while chewing a hamburger, particularly a molar, which Jamieson realized immediately would set him back at least a month's salary when his over fertile imagination added together a root canal (following cleaning and full mouth x-rays), a crown, and a new denture to accommodate the shiny metal clasps that, unable to be adjusted, necessitated a complete new upper partial which would embrace his restored tooth.

The alternative, an implanted metal device, screwed into his jaw that cost even more.

While these estate planning thoughts rushed through his head, he had the foresight to spit out the offending material that had caused such havoc in his mouth. He did a double take as a fully formed molar tooth landed on his plate. At first he thought that his own had been more than cracked, in fact completely dislodged, thus leaving a gaping hole in the back of his mouth, when he saw that the offending object had a neat hole drilled sideways through it, as if it had been strung, perhaps on a necklace. Such necklaces, he once read in a popular book purporting to tell the truth about tribes still hidden from civilization, suggested a cannibalistic society, where such objects were worn as trophies in place of shrunken heads once the warrior had collected too many to carry around his own neck.

How had it come to be in the hamburger, made from commercial pre-formed patties, claiming a stalwart pedigree of beef named after a Scottish blackguard, (my apologies to my friend Angus), he did not know. But which, like so many venerated heroes, had been morphed over the years into its current acceptable presentation, when in reality, it was composed of the worst in society in the case of the Scottish blackguard, or of offal and otherwise inedible bits of a beast with no genetic connection to an animal of breeding, in the case of the hamburger patty?

Did it fall from someone's barbaric piece of jewelry? If so, what had a cannibal been doing working in the meat packing industry? Or had the patty, dreadful thought of all dreadful thoughts, been made of ground beef which was in fact other cannibals, a more modern way of satisfying the diet while disguising the source.

Reaching into his pocket he dragged out his large bottle of gastric sedative, carried with him at all times for such drastic gastronomic emergencies, took a large swallow, burped, and summoned the waiter.

The waiter took one look at the offending foreign body that had set the scene for this confrontation, sighed, and fainted.

The manager rushed over, and while jabbering incomprehensibly in a tongue foreign to 99% of the customers, and the other 1% boasting of a fluency in a language they too did not comprehend, by body language and intonation, implied that Jamieson had floored the waiter with a sucker punch, and forthwith threw him from the premises with obvious threats of bodily harm if he returned.

Jamieson had the foresight to retrieve the drilled molar before leaving, having first squeezed his bottle of stomach lotion back into his pocket.

When he reflected later on his predicament, while constantly exploring his damaged tooth with his tongue, he decided that the manager could well be in on the whole enterprise, and could be the source of the hamburger meat.

However, to take his suspicions to the police would undoubtedly cause him to be examined under a section eight involuntary psychological examination, and probably condemned as a patient, and possibly even become a PhD subject for an upcoming anthropo/psycho/lawyeristic student, if he suggested that a local restaurateur could be a cannibal.

Although not apparent to Jamieson, his friends, if one could call them such because they tended to keep him in view when speaking to him, but at arm's length, guided by the friend with the longest arms, knew this man possessed an imagination that far outstripped his rational abilities to analyze and deduce, thus marking him as a fiction writer.

He sat, meditated, conjectured, ruminated and finally fell asleep, a quick release he frequently resorted to when faced with an imponderable problem such as a character in a story running amok and dragging the plot in an unidentifiable direction, which he felt fitted this situation.

As he napped, in that twilight between wakefulness and sleep, which the cognoscenti referred to as a hypnogogic state, when the visual imagination can produce flights of fancy worthy of a Timothy Leary trip, he imagined he boarded a plane to take him on a dental vacation to Costa Rica, where he could, for perhaps a third of the domestic price, have his mouth restored to its former condition. Unfortunately the flight was diverted unbeknown at that time to the passengers, who all seemed to have left except himself, and the plane shrunk from a wide-bodied commercial passenger plane to a small private two-seater that flapped its wings and relied on a single propeller to maintain its flying capabilities, and which landed in a clearing at the edge of a broad expanse of clear cutting in a tropical forest. He was met by a man with a feather through his nose, who grinning, explained in sign language that he intended to busy himself in Jamieson's mouth, then administered an anesthetic by pricking him in the rear, which he considered strange, he always used to having such injections in or near his gums.

He fought valiantly to escape before his remaining teeth were strung around his welcomer's neck, awakening, bathed in sweat, but with a clear need to prevent further escalation of the hamburger tooth incident, to find his rear irritated by the foreign tooth which he had placed in his back pocket.

Picking up a trusty spear, a souvenir of his dream, which was in fact an umbrella, he returned to the restaurant intending to rid the culinary world, and others with different interests, of this cannibalistic burden by using its poisoned tip with a quick thrust in any available spot on the manager's body.

His defense when the police arrived now seemed indefensible, considering the garbled story, a mixture of a foreign object, a drilled tooth, a dumb waiter, an incomprehensible manager, a grinning feather-bearing dentist, and a shrinking plane which flapped its wings. Particularly as he had used an umbrella in a threatening manner.

Some situations end well. Others badly. The call is often subjective. Jamieson was trapped either way. Fortunately, the two burly officers, armed to the teeth with more potent offensive weapons than an umbrella with a imaginary poisoned tip, happened to recognize him from a recently published book, which had documented the inevitable decline in mental abilities in the law enforcement field due to poisoning with blue dye from uniforms manufactured overseas, and using a dyestuff cheaper, though more lethal, than the domestic product used until the police outsourced its clothing requirements.

They were thus conflicted, due to not being sure how much of the story of the lethal dye was true, and how much imagination or bullshit.

They viewed his present explanation the same way, but decided that as the story had not yet been written, but intended to use flights of fancy that far outpaced the police procedural, they were intrigued to find out where it would go, and into whose ears it would reach, and whether the government would step in to ban hamburgers.

Thus Jamieson found himself back on the street, still nursing a cracked tooth, not daring to incur the wrath of a possible cannibal by suing for dental distress, but free of charges of assault or defamation of character, while being assured of at least two customers when his new book, if he ever lived to write it, was published.

As he left the restaurant he stuck out his tongue at the owner, who with a slight grin was busily tying together the ends of a necklace.

The Primary Candidate

Michael Sebaceous Malone, Oily to his friends, or Slick Mick as he was known to the press corps would have been at home in a Medieval Court; he had that certain ability to dodge and weave to preserve his head, and the willingness to dispatch a rival with a well timed rumor. However, by a genetic quirk of fate caused by Darwin, he arrived into the modern political scene with a coat of Teflon, full of deviosity, with a mind-set worthy of Machiavellian strategery.

Niccolo Machiavelli, Italian, who wrote *The Prince*, not to be confused with Antoine de Saint Exupery, French, author of *The Little Prince*, (also published in Spanish, *con ilustraciones del autor*), authored all the devilish tricks of manipulation, known as politics, to which we owe so much. Slick Mick emerged from the womb with a fully fledged and operating political genome.

Drawing on examples from Slick Mick, we can now consider the characteristics necessary to hold political office, even the highest.

To protect the innocent the name is a *nom de guerre,* an assumed name, literally *war name.* His close friends, what few he has, call him Oily. He prefers Michael or Marvelous, despite it sounding less egalitarian, a word totally misunderstood by both sides. The press corps, the sentient part of government, always refers to him as Slick Mick.

In studying his meteoric rise, I have been able to raise my tax bracket by writing numerous blogs and scurrilous articles, and an unauthorized book. The following observations are from my notes.

Let me first state a fundamental claim of all politicians hoping to hoodwink the public into choosing them over any other scoundrel, particularly for the highest office. All politicians promise to lower taxes, create more social programs, balance the budget, and reform entitlements. So, it shouldn't matter who you choose. Having got that out of the way, we can now decide how they reach that point.

The common denominator of politicians of all persuasions is their ability to manufacture fictions, which they call promises, often made in generalities, which later bear no relation to achievements. These are announced with such sincerity that even their mothers would be fooled. All politicians claim what they *will achieve*, not what they might only *try to do*, or not, depending on their condescension for the voting public, hoping, like the Mikado, it is enough to say something *should be done* to consider it *already done*, or, at least, that the voters will consider it already done.

I witnessed Slick Mick's opponent in a particular political skirmish. Taking a page out of Mick's own playbook, *"I wasn't there but let me tell you exactly what happened."*

"Remember the story of the frog and the scorpion who promised not to sting the frog to death if he would carry him across the river? He stung him just before they reached the far bank. 'Why?' asked the dying frog. 'It is in my nature the scorpion replied.'"

"You equate me with the scorpion?" Slick was genuinely surprised. "You think me immoral?"

"There is no morality in politics, merely expediency. Your promises are lies."

"I do not lie. When *I* use a word, it means just what I choose it to mean—neither more, nor less. How others choose to hear it is their problem."

I declined to get involved in their discussion. He was using the Humpty Dumpty defense from *Through the Looking Glass,* and we know where HD ended up.

Mick went on to mention words including *is, sex, lips, WMD,* and *no new taxes*—well, that last was three, but once politicians start talking, they find it difficult to stop.

"You are wrong about me as the scorpion," he continued. "I would only sting the frog if it harmed me. Certainty of retaliation is the best defense. If an opponent knows there will be reprisals he is reluctant to attack."

"You have been known to verbally attack people, not what they stand for, before they even do anything to you."

"Of course. This is today's world. Reality TV and tabloid magazines. The public is more interested in people than policies, most of which they don't understand. They will remember what I tell them is bad about the person long after they have forgotten his vague promises."

They might have carried on the argument had Michael's opponent lived. Unfortunately he was found next day with two bullet holes in his head and a suicide note, thus joining the many close political advisors and friends who pass rather quickly, politics being a dangerous profession, a subject usually avoided in polite political circles, when you can find one.

No one questioned Slick Mick.

I asked him what he intended to do since he was never one to allow a crisis to go to waste.

He pointed out that his opponent took great pains to be politically correct, always, and the public didn't like it. "I can afford to avoid political correctness and the people love me for it."

"Someone from the public did this to him?" I asked.

"How do I know? I never met the man."

I thought it better not to mention that I had witnessed an exchange between them, or at least, I knew exactly what happened, as had several million people on television. He anticipated my withheld comment.

"You see? That's what I mean. I may have spoken to him, but I never met him."

There is no doubt that the art of controlling your fellow man while feathering your own nest has been drawing men and women to the flame of power since Niccolo codified the necessary techniques. He recognized, and in some cases endorsed, dishonesty and killing as normal and effective political actions, depending what you mean by *dishonesty* and *killing*—(add them to *is, sex, lips, WMD,* and *no new taxes*).

Usually a political death is not to be equated with bodily demise, but not in every case.

You doubt this? Google deaths around your favorite politician, especially those who say they do not condone violence.

There are in all leaders elements of the psychopath. They send men out to be killed. They expect a cadre of dedicated bodyguards to lay down their lives for them if necessary. And they have the power to free men from justifiable death with a pardon. This sense of total power gives them over their fellow persons has been labeled by Philip Zimbardo, the Lucifer Effect.

These concepts Slick Mick completely embraced. Indeed, as mentioned earlier, it lies in his jeans—genes, and sometimes outside them.

Although the term Machiavellian has been accepted as political deceit by those who really do not understand politics, some, Spinoza, and Rousseau for example, (upper class) have argued that Niccolo was a Republican (lower class), even though his writing has been inspirational to *"proponents of modern Democratic political philosophy,"* (no class). This illustrates the similar behavior of politicians of all stamps and persuasions and the justifiable confusion of those to whom they appeal for support. It also underscores why some consider Slick Mick blue, some, red, and others, chartreuse.

James I of England said in 1604, *"So there is no Commonwealth, or Bodypolitcke, how well governed, or peacable soever it be that lackes the owne popular errors, and naturally inclined corruptions."* Although he had in common with Slick Mick the assumption that he was divinely chosen to rule over his people, he obviously had doubts about the morality of rulers. Not a lot has changed in the intervening four centuries.

Naturally inclined corruptions or scandals, when unearthed, revolve mainly around two subjects: sex, and fraud.

The former is perplexing and must be a carry-over from Genesis or the Puritans, since sex has been around longer than politics, perhaps you recall hearing of Adam and Eve, or Mark Anthony and Cleopatra? Long before Gary Hart, Willie the Wiener, and many others. In fact, most everybody does it sometime or another. Of course, not always with members of the opposition or their spouses. Or someone from a foreign embassy. Fraud is more difficult to prove since when one person is accused, the others look over their shoulders, pale into silence, or scurry away.

Slick thinks today's electorate should tolerate such minor indiscretions. "What is wrong with the public?" he asked rhetorically."We've always accepted that interns and insider trading are perks of the job. We have few enough of them."

We live in a democracy. James Russell Lowell said that "Democracy gives every man the right to be his own oppressor." So, we ourselves choose those who will exploit us. It has also been said, not least by Slick Mick in his most bombastic mood, that the truth will out at the ballot box, they will all vote for me! This is because if the other candidate, says it, hints it, supports it, or does it, it's bad, subversive, a lie, and he should be ashamed. If Slick says it, hints it, supports it, or does it, it shows his remarkable grasp of enlightened policy.

Unfortunately for the naïve voter, to expect reform by those who govern and have established the status quo is like asking the fox to secure the henhouse.

Slick Mick's epigenome, the part of his DNA that switches genes on and off, is affected by the environment, and is carried forward into subsequent generations. It governs his inherited behavior, which has been affected, altered, and directed through the ages by Feudalism, Revolution, War, his Privilege, Class Warfare, the voting Franchise, Reward, Exploitation, Greed, and the philosophy of "Get yours in first, chum. Alltime!"

Therefore, as a politician, his imbalance can be understood; not forgiven. He rouses us with fear, hope, and the promise of retribution, "Let's get 'em," thus using the voter as his hatchet man.

The voters, also inheritors of the same philosophies, may have been in addition subject to Exploitation, Slavery, Oppression, and countless False Promises of their leaders, and Privilege (not their own). So used are they to political rhetoric that they cynically answer to the one with the loudest voice, the most outlandish promises, and the one whose policies best pander to them—this Oily will say he didn't realize, while his Slick Mick persona doubles down—although his split persona appears conflicted how much either should promise as free stuff. That includes tax write-offs, and enough subsidies to satisfy all camps.

Slick even ignores the movement to change the term *deniable culpability* to *culpable deniability*. If politicians say they didn't do it, they are guilty, just read their lips, to coin a new political slogan. They should first check old news reports, using a blameworthy and disposable employee, before making such statements, particularly television clips. Once in office, the politician is able to hide behind any failed or unintended promise by sponsoring a bill that he knows will be voted down by colleagues. This helps any politician lay the blame on the true culprit—others. Slick feels his mastery of blunt language will save him here.

Politicians do *deals* on every subject, with themselves, their colleagues, the opposition, other countries, dictators, self-appointed Emperors, and the wealthy looking for favors. Slick feels he holds the trumps in any house of cards. These deals are known as *compromises*, which are only made if they benefit the politician himself. Many are kept secret from the public, which the administration purports to serve, since some have been known to foment riots, assassination attempts, and mass emigrations. With the latter Slick Mick concurs, although he privately prefers that emigration should be voluntary and ethnically selective.

They also serve on committees to spend your money, which of course are deals.

Slick Mick, while claiming to be an outsider, and thus naïve in political intrigue, has the necessary attitude and is a quick learner.

Politicians advance through the power of language. They use it persuasively in campaigns, argue vehemently in debates, and hallucinate on the floor of the house where they think they are saying something of value. Political speech is *largely the defense of the indefensible, "He wasn't dead, just non-viable."*

Slick Mick has yet to embrace all the available techniques of argument such as the euphemism; *innocent civilian targets are collateral damage due to incontinent ordinance.* Later he might learn gobbledygook, overpowering the target audience with bigger words and longer sentences, sometimes with an excuse, *"I guess I should warn you, if I turn out to be particularly clear, you've probably misunderstood what I said."*

He will undoubtedly use the mollification, such as saying that a lay-off initiates a career enhancement program. Closer to home, some of you may have bought pre-owned, experienced, cars, some of which are certified as such, which helps you to understand this technique.

In addition there are the evasion, the turn back, and the side-step to be used in debate, or the twist, *"We have nothing against ideas. We're against people spreading them."*

Confusion is part of the process.

"I intend to open this country up to democracy and anyone who is against that, I will jail."

"I plan to give leaders of the failed coup a fair trial, and then shoot them."

Iran executed thousands in 1981. Khomeini said *"those who prevent moral purification must be eliminated. In appearance this can seem like a mass killing to people, but in reality, it amounts to getting rid of obstacles to humanity—Iran purifies them if it can, or if not, it eliminates them."*

There is also the quickstep used to dance around several subjects at once. Slick at first sticks to the simplicity of denial, or calling everyone else a liar.

These techniques have a long history, and are part of the rite of passage for any political aspirant. As W S Gilbert wrote in *Patience,*

His meaning doesn't matter if it's only idle chatter of a transcendental kind.
And everyone will say,
As you walk your mystic way,

"If this young man expresses himself in terms too deep for me, why, what a singularly deep young man this deep young man must be!"

Liars fear looking guilty above all else. The rate of blinking is proportional to the depth of guilt. Therefore liars attempt not to blink, so the worst offenders are, paradoxically, those who do not blink at all. This can be easily verified on television news on the rare occasion when they show someone other than Slick—who never lies— particularly candidates of the feminine persuasion who blame false eyelashes and mascara. This is a compromise term which can apply to both genders. Had I said male or female, I would be considered sexist, a term Slick has been known to confuse with sexy.

Since applying Machiavellian principles (ha!), politicians have become identifiable through certain characteristics. All use an extensive vocabulary of redundancies and tautologies.

"There is not an upright man on two feet who cannot relate to a quadripedal four-legged canine dog," said Slick Mick, when he promised to support the Animal Rights Bill, which he championed for those who had no other form of health care.

"And once it is passed, you can read it and find out what I said."

Selective memory is a requisite, as is mastery of the Flip-Flop, which goes along with selective memory, and is denied vehemently.

The ability to select and press the right buttons for any desired effect, particularly at rallies and town hall meetings, gives any candidate a clear advantage. He can thus generate calm acceptance (rare), riots, TV sound-bites, and others.

Most, sensitive to the way the public view their exploitation of the electorate, labeling them *The Establishment,* claim to be outsiders, although often vague about being outside of what.

The ability to identify grievances and promise to redress them is a gift. If none can be found, Slick has been known, like his colleagues, to tell the public what they should have a grievance about.

Promises are couched in generalities, never to be tied to specifics. This is especially true in advocating foreign policies which we would label genocidal if used by foreign regimes.

Most have the ability to obfuscate with language. To some this comes naturally. Others have first to master the language of administrative Double Speak, a destructive language technique identified by George Orwell by which politicians *"bastardize the rules of language, obfuscate meaning, and distort understanding with hyperbole and euphemism."* Slick came to campaigning with a background in advertising and the particular use of words dedicated to *"undermining our understanding."* Nathaniel Hawthorne got this one right: *"Words – so innocent and powerless as they are, as standing in a dictionary, how potent for good and evil they become in the hands of one who knows how to combine them."* His comments are considered subversive.

Books and courses are readily available on the subject, written by close presidential advisors and spokespersons, to train the inarticulate in the art of political language, which. . . *"with variations (this) is true of all political parties, from Conservatives to Anarchists—is designed to make lies sound truthful and murder respectable, and to give the appearance of solidity to pure wind."*

And finally, the secret weapon, the ability to avoid being caught, which is of course their Eleventh Commandment, or, if caught, to believe their own denials.

Other common faults: are to believe, or disbelieve, what they themselves say, to operate on polls not convictions, to deny contradictions which never happen—*"There will be no carbon tax under a government I lead, but let's be absolutely clear. I am determined to price carbon."*

They all have an agreement to spend taxpayer money on a large corps of excuse makers, explainers, spokespersons; to make trips, the further, the better, in the interests of constituents; to have multiple skeletons in closets (often in boudoirs, banks, or hidden in freezers); a preference for pork over the real meat of any matter, and claims of many, many, attempts to stride cross the aisle, when they suddenly develop a short leg.

Presidents seldom criticize too harshly the failed promises of their predecessor, particularly if one manages to replace himself thus earning a second term, because the administration will inherit the problems which they failed to resolve.

I might point out the following adroit semi-truth—by saying they are denying the military their ability to interrogate prisoners of war, and then quietly outsourcing the procedures to Black Sites in other countries. When this raised a diplomatic howl worldwide, they decided to transfer such war prisoners, who are not bound by criminal law, to U.S warships where the High-Value Detainee Interrogation Groups could deal with them—17 ships at one count. So camps could be closed, not the interrogation process ended. The latter is, I believe, what the public understood would happen. The bad guys can still be captured and held indefinitely as enemy combatants. But the promise is fulfilled—case closed. Choose your explanation, the euphemism, mollification, the evasion, the turn back, the sidestep, or any combination thereof.

Slick comes prepared to overcome this problem; "My plan to redress this iniquity will be applauded when those behind bars, and those in front of bars, will no doubt realize that no one, I repeat no one, has produced such a solution, which in the view of most, is an enlightened solution to an insurmountable problem, and reduces the problem to one of semantics by upholding the second amendment."

Unless they can do it by dominating the news media, why do Slick Mick, and all political aspirants, spend so much to be elected? Because they hope to join the political elite, an oligarchy which can be seen battling courageously with opponents on behalf of constituents and others, while in private patting each other's backs for their brilliance in hoodwinking the country.

Niccolo spent most of his book advising princes how to battle other princes and giving not a fig for the people. Our politicians, and Mick, aim messages at the Middle Class, because the majority of the voting public does not like to be thought of as snobs by being called an Upper Class, and are insulted to be classified as Lower Class. Also if they are labeled Upper Class, it is assumed they are filthy rich from exploiting the masses, and if labeled Lower Class, it is assumed the taxpayer pays everything for them. Therefore everybody is happy to be called Middle Class, a meaningless term which is, of course, a compromise.

Many politicians are lawyers which gives them an advantage. They are able to argue for either side without any personal ideology or moral conviction. They have also given real lawyers a bad name.

Bob Woodward reminded Slick Mick that Campaigning is not the same as Governing, as he explained in *The Price of Politics,* but narcissists have selective hearing, and they believe themselves over anyone else. In fact voters cannot make politicians keep their promises. A ruling in a

New York court (O'Reilly v. Mitchell). *"Politicians are free to say whatever they want during an election campaign and then do whatever they want once in office."*

Slick Mick, and his colleagues, ignore in their reform rhetoric that the country is largely governed by the "Submerged State," which is hidden from prying eyes, and controls or rewards activities through tax breaks. For example those who want the government to keep their hands off *"my Medicare,"* not realizing it is a government program, outsourced to private insurers to do the government work for a remarkable profit—check their share prices—or believing that student loans are provided in a free market by altruistic banks when, under a compromise, the government guarantees the banks against default and subsidizes the interest payment with our money. However, this will all disappear with a flat tax—(ya think?)—including all the breaks Slick Mick and his wife and colleagues dearly love which are too numerous to list covering some 8000 pages. They may later reveal they meant "Modified Flat Tax," where each politician has the choice of 'a save' for their favorite exception, or two, or three.

The successful politician is also wary of the contingent promise; you scratch my back, and I'll scratch yours, which can devolve from scratching to the shaft.

Slick Mick is not immune to the promotion of political slogans that sound wonderful, often the idea of others, such as Flat Tax, Lower Tax, Tax the Rich, Make us Healthy again, Whole Again, Unite the Billionaire Class, and Enslave the Workers, and Import Cheap Labor so they are not seen to be exporting jobs.

There you have it. Why candidates work so hard, and spend so much to join the elite, and the necessary qualities of character (ha!), while TV companies laugh as this is where most of our political contributions wind up. They too believe in a profit motive.

Remember on the rare occasion when a politician retires, he or she is hardly destitute, seeing as they are paid for life, and often have well padded skeletons secreted in boudoirs, banks, or hidden in freezers.

Had Niccolo guessed how his stratagems would be seized, developed, and exploited, he might have claimed a pre-humous Nobel. His advice has blossomed into Political Science—that should tell it all. And Michael Sebaceous Malone revels in it all like a pig in slop.

Except where Malone is speaking, statements in italics are taken from politicians.

References:

The Prince, Niccolo Machiavelli, New York, Appleton Century Crofts, 1947

El Principito, (*Le Petit Prince*), Antoine de Saint Exupery, (Spanish translation, Buenos Aires 1953), New York, Harcourt Brace, 1973

Counterblaste to Tobacco, James 1, London, Rodale Press, 1954

The Submerged State-How Invisible Government Policies Undermine American Democracy, Suzanne Mettler, Chicago, The University of Chicago Press, (e-book)

His Own Oppressor, B.G. Paver, London, Peter Davies, 1958

The Price of Politics, Bob Woodward, New York, Simon and Schuster, 2012

Black Sites, Internet Search.

Double-Speak, William Lutz, New York, Harper Collins, 1990

Politics and the English Language, (Essay), George Orwell, 1946. For the Polish translation of this essay, which might be easier to understand:
http://www.autoteiledirekt.de/science/george-orwell-polityka-i-jezyk-angielski-1946

Translocation

If Wendell had not stuck a fork into an electrical socket at the age of four he would probably not have wanted to become an electrician. He rushed to his mother with joy on his face to show her how he had invented a new game where he could translocate himself from one end of the hallway to the other in the blink of an eye. She was not amused, but a cautionary mother if ever, she rushed out to the local discount store and replaced all her flatware with plastic.

Wendell was distraught. To an inventive and imaginative child, losing the first great step forward in his hoped-to-be entrepreneurial life, not that he had a clue that such a future was his for the mere action of living, was a threat. Henceforth he would not tell his mother, and especially her friends who gathered on certain mornings to share coffee and gossip, after they had found that one day he had substituted burnt peanuts for coffee beans. Since then they all observed him with wary eyes filled with trepidation, and those who failed to clutch their purses closely to their swollen bosoms had learned to check them for frogs and spiders before they left. Only one had been hospitalized for a Black Widow bite, but she had survived. This surprise result intrigued the young boy.

He needed a substitute for a fork. His fingers were too large, but he reasoned, within the limited capabilities of a four-year-old, even one as advanced with diabolical ideas as

Wendell, that the claws of their somnolent cat might work as well, he having no idea of the metallic requirement for the conduct of electricity, although flesh substituted quite well when required. This time he had no need to tell his mother. She responded to the smell of scorched keratin, the substance that comprised the nails, and used a word that Wendell would not learn for years to come. She wondered how the cat had lost most of its whickers, save for a few, small, twisted and coiled wisps where it had formerly proudly sported a bristling fan-like growth on each side of its face.

Strangely, and obviously protected by a supernatural force, his mother and the ageing cat survived his childhood, well, for at least two more years, and apart from a few minor fires and breakages, so too did the house.

By the age of seven, he taught himself by mistranslating do-it-yourself books, and having a fondness for colors, that electricity consisted of white volts and black volts—the black ones were the only ones capable of the phenomenon of relocation—occasionally red volts, which when added to black held a fascinating power when touched to the white volt wire, and of course, the rather useless green volts, which drained everything away, spilled them on the ground, at least that what he thought the books said, and spoiled all the fun.

He found his novel ideas subject to rejection by his physics teacher who Wendell decided must be taught the error of his beliefs before he corrupted yet another generation of students. He was annoyed at first that so few of his classmates shared his fascination with electrical power, they being content to turn lights on and off and allow their mothers to use it for cooking, probably because they were only six. He grew into the belief that as no one else was interested, he could proceed without interference, the physics teacher having disregarded his approach.

This disregard arose from two concerns. Wendell, at seven years of age, was several years from mathematics and physics and thus the physics teacher could afford to avoid the subject, pre-occupied as he was by courting Wendell's mother.

When Wendell saw the illustration of an electric chair, nicknamed Old Sparky, a term that fascinated him as he yet to give personal names to any experimental contraption he devised, he believed it pointed the way to the ultimate translocation device. He was further convinced of this by seeing that the subject was restrained by straps so they could not fly sway.

Finding an old chair in the garage, seldom frequented by his mother, and filled with a variety of materials valued by Wendell, termed junk by his mother, left behind by his father, Wendell fashioned a reasonable likeness of Old Sparky and powered it by using his favorite black and red volts. This may have sufficed for Old Sparky's designed intent, although far short of the voltage usually expected by those who threw the switch on the real thing.

He was at first perplexed about the choice of an experimental subject. The cat was too squirmy, and the dog far too restless to hold either in the chair's restraints. However, the house next door housed a young girl, who Wendell had found to his satisfaction, would do most things he asked for ice-cream.

He had her, ice-cream in hand, ensconced in the chair, when his mother chose to show her new beau over the house, which included the garage. The horror was mutual. Mother and her beau expected to witness an electrical *translocation*, which they believed meant to the next world, and Wendell appalled that he was about to unintentionally reveal his new findings to an adult who had laughed and made fun of his enquiry for knowledge.

Neither happened. The little girl was able to finish her ice cream none the wiser for her proximity to the afterlife. The other three were at a stalemate.

Wendell had not actually committed anything. The circuit, although prepared, had not been completed. Mother wished to play down the delinquency of her son so as not to scare away a potential mate, and he, like the small male about to be eaten by his larger black widow female, was reluctant to reveal to her that the experiment carried the danger of death, so as not to use her son to poison her against him. And he was loathe to report the incident to the authorities, so as not to alienate his, hopefully, soon-to-be mate.

They reached a compromise agreed by all. Wendell's mother relinquished her custody of her child to his father who had for long been agitating for just such an action. This resolved her of responsibility. Her beau breathed a sigh of relief that he had no firm decisions to make, and Wendell was ecstatic since his father, probably still accumulating junk, had no idea of his son's brilliance, nor of his interest in translocation.

He unfortunately discovered it one night when Wendell, annoyed at the frequent garage inspections by his father trying to take an interest in his son's activities, had transformed his bed as a bier to the afterlife. Suspicion is not proof. Wendell's innocence prevailed, since all clues and evidence were destroyed in the subsequent fire. Father was lucky to escape, unfortunately with a severe memory loss, although convinced his survival was due to his son, and praising him for what he considered, a daring rescue.

Wendell was now free to take the next step on his path.

The Muse and a Rose

"My horse for a writing prompt," I cry to my absent muse.

Perhaps my writing muse can't stand horses.

I am in midstream; dare I change?

I glance at a list of several articles to write, some in outline form. They do not press any creative buttons. So, fearful that I face the cruel sentence (sic) of uncreative silence, I pick up a book to check it against the criteria with which I punish myself for reading like a writer. That is, to answer how a successful author, one who has not only written, but been published, deals with questions of character, conflict, setting, tone, dialogue, and all the myriad components of a story, hoping he will spare a crumb of creativity seeing as my muse apparently has no intention of helping me.

The first question, will the story engage me?

I choose a book written in 1930, the classical and definitive history of Britain, *1066 and All That*, by W.C. Sellar and R.J. Yeatman, subtitled *A Memorable History of England*.

I am immediately engaged because it stirs memories of archived history lessons, whose Dewey Decimal classification is no longer subject to my recall.

In terms of characters, settings, and events, the interpretation and spelling of Messrs. Sellar and Yeatman presents a challenge to the serious reader of history, for whom this book is clearly not written. Until now, I have not been a serious student of history.

The authors, quite rightly they feel, claim that British history started in 55 BC the year Julius Caesar landed at Thanet in England. *"The Scots (originally Irish but by now Scotch) were at this time inhabiting Ireland, having driven the Irish (Picts) out of Scotland; while the Picts (originally Scots) were now Irish (living in brackets) and vice versa."*

Within a few paragraphs we have the promise of the book, the tone, the voice, and definitive characters in conflict. They have captured me.

The Romans eventual departure *". . . to take part in Gibbon's Decline and Fall of the Roman Empire. . . left Britain defenseless and subjected Europe to that long succession of Waves of which History is chiefly composed. . . Britain was attacked by Waves of Picts, (and of course, Scots) . . . and of Angles, Saxons and Jutes."*

In very short order we have the setting: Britain full of early Brits many of whom were reputed to paint themselves blue (probably the cold). Characters in conflict: Romans who had reached the limit of their straight roads, versus the rest, Picts and Scots who couldn't quite decide who they wanted to be, and Angles, Saxons and Jute refugees. The particular epic journey facing them all: The Wave interpretation of history, each sinusoidal turn threatening to vanquish everyone by fire and sword.

As each group was about to reach their goal, they were set back by another Wave of Antagonists who also interrupted Periods such as Ancient and Modern, Past and Present, Early-eval, Medi-eval, and Lately.

Would that I were able to so succinctly set the tone for my writing.

The catch twenty-two of attempting to read like a writer is the inborn fault of being a reader. Once I was engaged I couldn't put the book down, and thus blew a couple of hours on 'research'. It could be argued that I might have as easily roamed the warrens of cyberspace. The difference is that cyber-searches tend to be diffuse, branching, and interminable. Fortunately a book is focused, right to hand, and can be carried along to the bathroom.

If there is a shortcoming to this book, as with all establishment histories of Britain, including this one, it is to ignore the dramatic effect of cuisine. A deficit I feel compelled to correct before considering the rest of the book such as beginning, middle and end, and character arcs. As an impending student of history herewith are a few corrections and new pointers to the evolution of that overcrowded island shrouded in mist and, as far as native behavior goes, mystery.

You are what you eat, or what has eaten you.

Contrary to the belief of pizza lovers, it is not widely known that the Romans expected to win over the people with pasta, since pizza had yet to be invented by Americans who had yet to be invented. The Brits, who had no equivalent for pasta, in word or food, believed it grew on trees and never got the harvest dates right. They settled for small pieces like chopped worms drowned in tomato sauce in cans introduced (later) by the Americans, once they had been invented, as payback for George III opposing afternoon tea.

Because they had no tomatoes until Columbus was discovered by America (which was not yet invented) Italian pasta was bland and best left on the trees.

This confusion over diet persisted until William the Conqueror invaded in 1066 and introduced French words to separate the Norman invaders from the indigenous peasants (and nobility). This they did by introducing unpronounceable menus. However, they allowed the Brits to continue using their own words for animals on the hoof, which they couldn't pronounce, but insisted on French terms for meat on the table, which the Brits couldn't pronounce. They probably did it in other areas too, but I didn't have time to be sidetracked.

The stew of Brits, Picts, Scots, Romans, Saxons, Angles, and Jutes was further thickened by Normans and Danes, and then seasoned with West Indians, Pakistanis, Iraqis and other spicy middle easterners who arrived in the inevitable Waves. From it emerged a British Diet which no one liked because it was tainted by everyone else until the battle was won by the Pakistanis and Indians who curried everything. The native diet of overcooked beef, over-boiled potatoes, mushy peas and tasteless cabbage, or the Scot offering of Haggis, didn't stand a prayer. Chicken Tikka Masala, and Chicken Jalfrezi are now recognized as fundamental English dishes alongside the two remaining native English dishes, the Mixed Grill, and Fish and Chips. When Basmati rice superseded the Irish potato, the fate of British cuisine was sealed. As was the country.

An army may march on its stomach, but this is the first record of a nation conquered by food. This might be worthy of a PhD thesis. Sellar and Yeatman can be forgiven for this omission as their book predated the cooking channel by about 75 years.

Everyone also had to drink. The natives drank warm British beer. This delayed the invention of America which eventually countered by inventing ice. The Church fostered ale houses because beer was safer than water and drunk with every meal. Brits who could afford it could drink mead, (fermented honey) if they wanted a real buzz. The Romans drank wine, a habit that persists at cultural literary soirees and, the more mundane, writing-function cocktail hour.

Beer and chai were introduced to India by Brits. And they got more of their own back after being conquered with curry by stealing a lot of Indian words and teaching them cricket.

Meanwhile, back a wave or two, sometime after the Romans left to help Gibbon, the Saxons arrived. *"The brutal Saxon invaders drove the Britons westward into Wales and compelled them to become Welsh."*

Fortunately they didn't develop a national Welsh cuisine, or if they did, it has been forgotten except for Welsh rarebit, (pronounced rabbit) which has nothing to do with bunnies, and everything to do with cheese. Maybe it got lost in the translation of all those Welsh consonants.

They re-emerged into the limelight, yearning for a good steak, when the House of Lancaster decided to pelt the house of York with roses, the English and Welsh being gentle souls and nations of gardeners, as they would have you believe.

Following 1066, British history had progressed through invasion, occupation, slaughter, and displacement causing battles for the throne which make present day elections pale into insignificance. Not having bingo or TV, the disgruntled nobility had to make their own Waves.

History gets more confusing when the first horticultural battle over an inedible flower (because of thorns), divided the country some 400 years after the Norman invasion. Henry, of the house of Lancaster, from Wales, which was known as Tudor, battled for the throne against Richard of the house of York, who was known as King, over the color of a rose. To confuse things further, they were both of the Plantagenet family, which means they shared a mitochondrial Eve. They were also both Catholic, so both had the same second in their corner.

Henry won the day and went on to become King, and to found the highly successful Tudor house, a design still popular today. Richard III wound up dead under a parking lot in Leicester. Sir Walter Scott can take credit for naming their conflict the War of the Roses in 1829, based on a scene in Shakespeare's Henry VI Part I, which does not refer to the winner who was Henry VII. Go figure. However, thanks to the Bard, the five sovereigns of the Tudor dynasty are among the most well-known figures in Royal history.

There is no record of whether the roses were Multiflora, Floribunda, or Polyanthus. I grow Red Knock Out roses as a hedge, red. The red roses represented the winning side, the Tudors, Welsh. Well, my grandmother was reputed to be Welsh, so that's appropriate.

A War of Roses sounds benign, a battle of petals and thorns, but they were backed by sword, mace, club and arrow, and the dreaded halberd, with which, researchers suspect, a Welshman, landowner Rhys ap Thomas, sliced off the back of Richard's skull at the battle of Bosworth, thus sparing Henry the trouble, after he, Richard, had made a mad charge on horseback at his adversary.

The halberd was a fearsome weapon—an axe blade topped with a spike mounted on a shaft five or six feet long. It also bore a hook to yank unfortunate horsemen from their mounts. Check out the Swiss guards at the Vatican; they still carry them in preference to M16's.

If Henry had not left Wales, probably in search of something more edible than cheese bunnies, that would have ended British history. However, Henry VII begat Henry VIII who begat Elizabeth I, and Bloody Mary.

Henry VIII, petulant over the Pope's refusal to let him divorce, decided his subjects ought to follow the belief of Martin Luther, a German polymath cleric (monk, theologian, professor, and priest), rather than the Pope who up to then, not being married, had no idea what cooping up a man and woman together for life could do. At the time, Henry believed his decision to be the most convenient. He pronounced himself Head and Defender of the Faith (whichever he chose) which proved to be quite unnecessary as he subsequently found it far easier to chop off the head of a displeasing wife, which saved a lot of political and religious hassles.

Elizabeth sent Sir Walter Raleigh to America, which had by then been found, to bring back tobacco which turned out to taste worse than spinach and was only good for heating small pipes. However, entrepreneurs convinced the population that breathing the smoke would cure ailments from lumbago to wens and warts (ancient afflictions) thus stimulating the casket industry.

Around about then, the Spanish, whose history we are less interested in, started importing from Mexico, a subject which became a Hot Potato. This caused Ireland. And the tomato, which revived the Romans into Italians and let them build a wall around the Pope's house.

Mary, in the interests of leaving her mark on British cuisine, introduced the barbecue, first practicing on 300 Protestants. Later both sides ganged up on bad cooks, called witches, and cured them of their heresy by tying them to stools and dunking them in village ponds as if they were rinsing Basmati rice.

When I was old enough to recognize stuff, I found I was Protestant, although I had no idea what I was protesting, only that the Head of State, the Queen, was C. of E. and head of the church. My future wife was Catholic, so the descendant of Luther's nemesis would not accept our marriage as sanctified by his God, who I thought was the same one the C. of E. recognized. Anyway, to satisfy both pathways to salvation, my wife and I had a renegade Franciscan monk bless our union, and a local judge to stand in for the priesthood and pronounce us man and wife.

In much the same way, in a spirit of compromise, the winner of the rose contest, Henry VII, then married

Elizabeth of York, but as everyone was Catholic at the time, they had no need for a Justice of the Peace, (an odd title for someone who marries people), and they united the kitchens of both houses to preserve Lancashire Hotpot and Yorkshire Pudding.

The skeleton of Richard III, who came second with the white rose, was recently exhumed from a parking lot in Leicester, in England, which of course wasn't there when he was buried. Instead it was a Franciscan Priory. So I guess Franciscan monks, probably not renegade, carried out his funeral.

Strangely, his bones, not his stomach, revealed he confused the Culinary Waves and fed "on a high end diet of fish, swan, crane and heron, and a vast quantity of wine." The soil below his skeleton proved he had been infested with roundworms, suggesting that he may have made his dramatic charge at Henry due to an itchy bum.

Food also contributed to the Renaissance which chased away the Dark Ages after the horticultural battle was acknowledged to be the end of the Medieval Period. Architects learned to drop straight lines from a plum. Newton learned gravity from an apple before switching to figs, although apples set back medicine for years by keeping doctors away, and we are still investigating its effect on education as teachers have, over the years, been the largest consumers of Granny Smith, John McIntosh, Harrison, and their other relatives.

I may, or may not, add a later footnote about peripheral eating fads such as Chinese, German, Italian, and the persistent French. But many have been superseded by McDonalds, an American outfit hiding behind a Scottish name, which was recently reported to be considering mounting a challenge to the Indians with a MacHaggis. It is doubtful if it will survive uncurried. However the Scots also invented Whiskey as an alternative to Mead to keep the cold away which led to Golf where you beat your opponent's balls with a club, which they considered kinder than chopping off his head with a halberd.

Waves have ups and downs. Before the resolution of the Curry Wars, The British Diet, drove people from the misty island in Waves, and, together with being rudely told to take tea elsewhere by the Americans, who they had invented, (partially, mostly, completely—to avoid author bias, readers may choose their own adverb), led to Empire, a Reverse Wave. They avoided Europe because of the Diet of Worms, which the Pope made Martin Luther eat with his words, and because the only native European vegetable was the cabbage which they tried to disguise as cauliflower, broccoli, cabbage, Brussels sprouts, cabbage, and other *cruciferae* which made a serious contribution to global warming, although they didn't know they caused greenhouse gasses because the greenhouse had not yet been invented by garden stores.

In addition to the criteria of character, conflict, setting, tone, and dialogue, I also wanted to gain insight into how the authors dealt with the beginning, middle and end, and various arcs.

Britain had more history at the beginning (this the authors clearly demonstrated), which is in inverse ratio to the number of historians. This equation has persisted to the CE, current era, not to be confused with C. of E. The middle is somewhat confused due to the surge in Norse, Danish, and other unpronounceable names, and the balance of the end of British history is disturbed by the weight of differing opinions (historians again), and the end of the curry conquest, and is hence abrupt.

Meanwhile, the arc of British History is clearly visible, even without the irrational omission of the dramatic effect of cuisine, which I have now corrected.

Unfortunately, S and Y wrote their history in 1930 and hence ended British History prematurely.

"The Great War was between Germany and America and was thus fought in Belgium. . . the Americans being 100% Victorious."

This was, of course, repeated nine years later although the conclusion is unchanged.

"America was thus clearly top nation, and history came to a ." *(Full stop)*

Thankfully Sellar and Yeatman answered my call for the help I expected from a delinquent and absent muse. Not only did their treatment of history stimulate my hibernating writing passion, but now, as a serious student of history, it enabled me to achieve a measure of reflected fame by being able to correct their accidents of culinary ignorance.

There is no doubt that we sometimes need a different horse to carry us onward to overcome the sentence of uncreative silence. I empathize with Richard, despite his rich diet (glutton). He lost his horse, and Sellar and Yeatman provided mine.

Possibly **The End**, unless another cooking fad develops.

Postscript:

In case you think that the Brit-India association is not real, consider that Prince William, future English King, carries Indian genetic markers in his mitochondrial DNA that he inherited through an unbroken maternal chain six grandmas back. His horticultural interests remain a palace secret although I am convinced he likes curry; otherwise he wouldn't be British—or Indian.

The Selfie Generation

On the third Wednesday of the third month after she had bought her Z-phone model 6, Julie awoke, stretched, reached for the instrument and took a selfie. It had become a habit to snap pictures of herself whatever she was doing, wherever she was, as if to vindicate that she had been there. She did have scruples. She drew the line at selfies in the shower, but those that knew her, were aware this was not because of a moral clause in her living manifesto, simply that she did not want to damage her smart phone in the pouring water.

Her image smiled back at her. After gazing at it for a few moments she put down the phone and climbed out of bed. When she looked across the room she knew something was different. The room was static. When she moved her head, the picture didn't change. She had lost a sense of direction; everywhere she looked it was the same. On the verge of panic, she picked up her phone to text a friend. As she did so the world came back to life.

She shook her head, believing this was perhaps a lingering dream. She was normally not too swift to focus in the morning, there being a delay as her neurons came on line sequentially, usually most, sometimes not all.

After conquering the bathroom—as if she were a subject in a static picture, she not wanting to risk her phone by using it in the shower—she left it to the imagination of her friends to visualize the difficulties a blacked out toilette caused, she switched on her phone to dress and noticed the world growing dim. On the verge of panic, she saw that the battery was low. Hastily plugging into a charger, she dressed, attempting to do it at first with her eyes closed. When this proved difficult, and makeup impossible, she waited impatiently for the phone to recover some life before using it again. She soon learned that her visible world was limited to what the phone viewed no matter how she turned her head.

She then hazarded the stairs.

It was much liked trying to navigate wearing reading glasses, or so she imagined, she having always used contacts, the stair treads out of focus. The problem persisted unless she used the phone as her eyes. Distances had to be recalculated from the subconscious automatic guidance system to which she was so accustomed that she forgot that distances were distorted by the camera lens. She had only to save herself twice. She arrived at the base of the stairs with a heart rate 120% of normal, which of course, being anything if not modern, she considered a sign of a good cardiovascular workout.

Her brain appeared to have melded with her phone's view of the world. And, moreover, she found, when she turned on her phone, she must first snap a selfie before the view was activated, otherwise her visual cortex refused to accept what she expected it to see. Her own picture appearing to be a password to the world.

After she left the house she paused a moment to go online, had she not stopped she would have been walking blind.

Before that fateful Wednesday, she had run into trouble several times while texting as she walked. Once she smacked into a utility pole. On another occasion she ran into a car's fender and was only saved from death or mutilation by the fact the driver was paying attention and neither texting nor speaking on his cell phone. She once stepped into a pothole and sat down firmly on her behind whereupon she was challenged by a uniformed minion of the law that she was under the influence. She indeed was, but not of alcohol. Nevertheless he insisted she perform simple math tests in her head and recite the alphabet. He did not make her do it backwards. She failed both.

She insisted on a breath test while, of course, recording all on her smart phone.

The officer obliged. She was let go but not before she had two thousand hits on her selfie with the officer posted to the social media. Her audience were divided between those who believed she had done nothing wrong and should sue the city for its casual placement of utility poles and not repairing potholes, and those who laughed at her ridiculous appearance, over a fender, in a pothole on her sitty-down, or with a large noggin on her noggin, and said she should pay for the damage. Someone even suggested the city should sue her for damage to the utility pole. Who was to know whether the pole would fail in the future due to her head butt?

When she connected to the Internet, she found to her consternation and alarm that she had the same condition that; like an electronic affliction, was engulfing the world in a pandemic.

Apparently that very morning a tipping point had been reached. Once sufficient millions were tuned to their smart phones for all their activities, which they could not accomplish without photographing themselves in the picture, the world-wide communication network, programmed to follow the popular requests, composed the most logical branching network, and fused them together. Now reality and selfies were inseparable, and the smart-phone was the portal to this new existence.

The initial alarm can barely be imagined.

The patient's immediate reflex action was to text their friends, and spread their concern an all available social media, immediately burying cyberspace under an avalanche of data. Who could have thought that only twenty-six little shapes, which most had forgotten went by the name of alphabet letters, could lay to rest several million brains fused together in permanent electronic communication? The logjam caused some thousands to suffer from electronic constipation, and an equal number from electronic starvation. Gurus, geeks, and nerds were equally afflicted.

The event served to shake the entire global community. Rather like an earthquake alerting to the need for restructured buildings, so the world faced he comingling of humanity with electronics.

The fusion was limited. Although bound together, the amalgamated neural circuits of millions did nothing to enhance global computing power. This was attributed to the narrow focus of most of those fused together resembling a gigantic collage rather than a super computer.

The normal brain was not evolved for this, and the sudden evolutionary spurt forward showed that without power in their phones, they were trapped inside their own thoughts with no outside communication or navigation skills. Navigating through the maze of selfies became a task as daunting and frightening as swimming with sharks, which in a sense it resembled, since con-artists and so-called startup companies attempted to unload primitive navigation aids on the public. The clogged bandwidth prevented anyone save the big three or four companies from doing anything and as they were constantly peering in the mirrors of their own achievement, they made little progress in a backward direction to a reset position. This they were used to doing on a computer. Not with a human brain—millions of brains! Millions of narcissistic brains.

Conspiracy theorists proposed several scenarios of big brother designing the global pandemic so as to take ultimate control, but as many of the theorists, government burocrats, and senior electronic executives were as addicted to selfies as the public to whom they catered, the theories became tied up in red electronic tape.

All the government efforts, despite their best intentions, for themselves of course, foundered on the electronic logjam because no government program could be written simply, without several hundred amendments and attachments unrelated to the real purpose of the bill.

Pastors, gurus, counselors, psychologists, apologists, and massage therapists, were overwhelmed with requests for help, mental and physical. Unfortunately, their interactions were as constrained by the electronic logjam as their potential clients. Their hands were tied, felt most keenly by the massage therapists.

Lines developed at charging points. Disputes were self limiting. As phones died so did their users awareness. It took the activities of a sudden cadre of fully charged helpers to assist the electronically blind.

The minority who could still read, write, and understand grammar were delighted. Although handwriting had been downgraded and in many areas lost, the overwhelmed text services showed that reading was still all powerful—as long as it was on a smart phone or a tablet, and in tiny-tiny words and sentences. Some die-hards still owned computers, and those who always had their computer cameras on were quickly absorbed into the selfie-net, accepted into the community of the fused, and removed from the read/write minority.

Although the majority still buried themselves in tablets and smart phones no matter where they were, it was obvious they were frustrated not being able to communicate as they habitually did, and they provided endless amusement to the others trying to do everything while needing to point their phones.

Most, used to the abbreviated language of texting were unable to comprehend words, complete sentences, or, the overwhelming effort of mastering complete paragraphs. Since their schooldays, texting, unsupervised by parents and ignored as an expedient path to peace by teachers, had led to a population segment, growing larger by the minute, who their ancestors would have called, illiterate. Switch off the power and they were struck dumb.

Once the dust had settled, the world began to adapt to the new condition.

Class barriers of low, middle, and upper, based on a combination of socio-economic status, primarily wealth, were replaced by three different groups—the *an-intellectual group*, the *political group*, and, for want of a better term, the *cursive class* who had never been bound to an electronic crutch.

The narcissistic *an-intellectua* who had precipitated the crisis reveled in their prominent selfie status even as they had their voices stifled. As a late-night comic remarked, a selfie is worth a thousand texts.

The political class rapidly adapted. They constituted the one group who seemed to have escaped inconvenience. Politicians, used to being a focus of attention, found little difference with a phone view, and were flattered that their own likeness was required as a password to allow them to access any form of communication. This soon gave way to frustration when cyberspace was overwhelmed by texting and broadband devoted to data transmission was effectively reduced to a narrow spectrum. No politician welcomed having his speech cut short.

Governments around the world rose to the occasion. Most immediately imposed a tax on selfies and secretly programmed phones to automatically charge personal accounts and send the money to the IRS. If one was broke, one remained electronically silent. A value-added-tax was assessed on the length of text messages.

The cursive class, mixed in their feelings over their newfound status, and the responsibility that they alone could communicate on an intelligent level, not from any innate superiority, but because of their freedom from narcissistic constraints, were thus the only group capable of restoring sanity and combat the ruthless predations of an unrestrained political class.

They argued, as the intelligentsia is apt to do, over whether the solution was to be found in further progress, or by a reversal of the new selfie state. Some wrote learned papers which few read. Some formed committees and spent hours drawing up rules of conduct and responsibility.

The world, well, the part of it that urged correction who were not writing papers or serving on committees, craved pragmatists.

An urgent world conference of city planners considered the cost of changing all streets to run backwards and all traffic controls to point the other way, having the false idea that one should be actually taking a selfie while driving and thus drive backwards. The task was so enormous that it would take days. Sense prevailed when they realized it would be like changing the side of the street to drive on over a period of time, thus adding to the chaos of people travelling both ways simultaneously. They realized belatedly that the selfie acted only as a password.

An appeal was made to the CEO's of all social media platforms and all manufacturers of the diabolical devices that allowed most of the population to isolate themselves. They in turn pleaded the first to the umpteenth amendment for the right to personal privacy—quite ignoring the fact that the population was fused into the equivalent of a bagel, there were after all, two sides to everything— and refused to act. Possibly they couldn't, having been hoist by their own petard, because being forward thinkers as they were, they too were unused to doing anything to reverse progress.

Several solutions were banded about from viruses that would infect the phones and do nasty things to the images, to brainwashing squads. These were instantly seen as a potential growth industry. Several companies applied for start-up funds to all unaffected philanthropists.

Until the mind boggling fusion of minds and electronics had so confused everyone, the simple solution to most electronic problems had been forgotten. A ten year old offered the solution.

The secret was to do the computer equivalent of unplug. They needed to reboot or allow the batteries to run down completely and start over from scratch. Switch off, unplug, wait twenty seconds, and presto, and hope their brains followed suit. The only problem was to get everyone to do it at once or at least in large groups.

The ten year old offered further words of advice. "Do what my parents do," he said. *"They* unplug *me."*

Governments were now faced with a loss of their new source of revenue. However, many were growing tired of being one pea in a pod of several million. The possibility of elections swayed the political argument.

The electronic brain fusion, in response to the popular demand to spread selfies and texting was as responsive to the needs of others as stodgy bread pudding.

Once politicians found it difficult or impossible to spread their doctrines they caucused and argued face to face. Remembering the method taxed their memories.

Time for action.

The rolling blackout of midsummer caused numerous complaints and threats of suits, a fear of a later overwhelming increase in the birthrate, fears that new mothers would be unable to take selfies with their newborns, and the widespread fears of isolation as social communication would be limited.

In this they were partially correct.

An automatic switch to prevent any photographs, in fact any electronic communication being taken while moving in a vehicle, save for GPS location, went into immediate effect. Naturally a permit for any such action must be bought from, and issued by, the government. Remedial classes in writing and grammar were mandatory before a license to reactivate a smart phone would be given, and fines were instituted for anyone considered creating a direct threat against the state by walking into any public sign, utility pole, or pothole.

This whole fiasco served to temporarily save the postal service and helped the writing paper and envelope industry, so that no ill wind could be considered a nationwide catastrophe.

The most unfortunate side effect was the termination of several thousand emergency room doctors who were specialists in body/object collisions. Some, those who still possessed readable writing skills, set about writing five minute clinical guides to the diagnosis and treatment of selfie constipation, textual logorrhea, and numb finger tips.

On the third Wednesday, two months following her dramatic finding of her mind bending experience, Julie awoke from a dream and automatically reached for her cell phone to register a record of her awakening.

As she took a selfie, a virus infection compared her picture to a facial recognition software program and diverted her call to the shopping channel.

One of many entrepreneurs had found a way to cash in on reflex actions of the marginalized population. Locked into the shopping channel she found she could only restore her normal smart phone service by buying something. She chose a hand mirror.

The ten-year-old's solution was hailed as mind boggling. He was immediately summoned to the White House to textually chat with the President while they ate in quiet electronic isolation so neither would feel displaced. Several prestigious universities awarded the young man a PhD after they got over their embarrassment at being caught up in the confusion of electronic pathways, which like electrical cords stored neatly in a box, find a life of their own and entwine themselves into Gordian Knots.

The country yielded to the United and Semi-Communicable Nations by considering a Nobel Prize for the youngster.

Later recriminations over responsibility for the debacle, who should pay how much to whom and for what kept an entire population of international lawyers sleepless for weeks, it was decided that there was enough blame to spread globally that all litigation should be dropped. A few fleas on the hide of the industry persisted in worrying at the subjects until they electrocuted themselves and died a quiet death.

Epilogue

A baseball field was named after the boy, totally unrelated to his achievement, as was typical of governments, the Senator who proposed it having a large convenient piece of suitable land to sell to the government, and a large illuminated selfie of the young man was made a permanent fixture in Time Square.

Mud and Murder

Jimmy-the-Cosh considered himself above average in street smarts, but the frustration of being interrupted in the course of a murder, which forced him to double the body count, sorely tested his abilities. Two bodies increased his disposal and cover–up arrangements quite out of proportion to the extra deed, due to his intention to remove and dispose of the initial corpse on a motorcycle. This complicated an otherwise simple rub-out and quick disposal.

The two victims in question, a notoriously crooked bookmaker and his enforcer, would be no loss to the village. The pair had never been successfully prosecuted. Witnesses had a tendency to lose their memories, or find an urgent need to visit a distant relative without leaving a forwarding address. More than a few had required the urgent attention of the ageing sawbones who provided medical services, for a modest fee, and free to those in the racing trade. Some had disappeared completely.

There was a pale silver lining to this dark cloud. Jimmy-the-Cosh owned a vintage World War Two German-army motorcycle, complete with sidecar, designed to carry three soldiers into battle. He had intended his victim to ride in the sidecar. Now he must also use the pillion to accommodate the additional body of the enforcer who had so rudely interrupted his initial plan.

He placed the two bodies in positions visually reminiscent of life before driving off. The first he sat in the regulation sidecar, which was always attached to military motorcycles in a vain attempt to keep upright vehicles that their inexperienced riders constantly tried to lay down, the other corpse tied to the pillion seat and belted to himself in an effort to keep it upright.

Unfortunately the bodies swayed. This alerted a passing patrolman to consider the degree of sobriety of all three, and whether this could contribute to filling his roster of needed tickets, and earn his, usually missed, monthly bonus.

Jimmy responded immediately to the lawman's rapid pursuit. The swaying trio charged through the darkened streets. The staccato roar of a motorcycle engine past its prime and running on one fewer cylinders than its design specifications, shattered an otherwise silent early morning. The patrolman adding to the disturbance with the police car's horrendous flashing lights and siren, which he had forgotten how to turn off.

Jimmy shouted epithets at the policeman, and encouragement to the corpses to "hang in there," until he reached their intended destination, a bridge over the river from which the village took its name. Serenity.

The quick and quiet disposal had become a complicated game.

Taking advantage of the narrow width of the motorcycle, and its ability to survive attempts to maneuver it in tight places, Jimmy managed to elude the patrolman. While Jimmy was able to discharge his cargo over the bridge, the unfortunate patrolman later faced the anger of the town council and the remaining citizens for his breach of the peace.

Having had a dry summer, the river was low enough to reduce the usually robust flow of water to a thin stream, meandering between stagnant pools exploited by breeding mosquitoes. Jimmy had neglected to keep up to date on such banal current affairs as drought, and so it happened, that his post-mortem burdens, launched from a height, both stuck headfirst in a recently exposed mud bank, like two unexploded WWII bombs, matching his motorcycle in age, their legs rising into the air, being rapidly fixed in position by rigor mortis, looking like overfed fins to explosive ordinance, one with shoes, one without.

Thus were they found next morning.

The patrolman, on being alerted to the finding of two unexploded bodies the following day, was delayed in his arrival due to writing a ticket, and a lengthy statement, for his own crimes—breach of the peace, shattering the sound ordinance, and waking the mayor's rooster who had the neighbors wake well before their habitual hour.

When confronted with the corpses he called on the fire service for help in hosing down the bodies so as to facilitate identification, should one be possible. They carried their own supply of water with them in a large fire-red truck, and thus had no need to further drain the river.

Patrolman, firemen, and Mayor gathered knee deep in mud, contemplating the spectacle, with not one of them eager to identify the dead, as this would suggest that they were familiar with the gentlemen and their profession.

Meanwhile, Jimmy-the-Cosh, believing that a brazen showing would assure everyone that he had nothing to do with the muddied bodies, parked his motorcycle outside the local Discount Feed, Weed and Coffee store, and, while drinking his highly caffeinated breakfast, was alarmed to see a concerned citizen, the wife of the deceased bookmaker, bending over his sidecar. When she straightened herself, she waved a pair of shoes in her hand and screamed that she had found the hearse. This was discounted by the authorities since none of them could remember ever seeing a motorcycle hearse.

The patrolman, firemen and Mayor, after a brief mutual board meeting of the Serenity Safety Committee, decided that someone who waived shoes about claiming she knew the feet they were ripped from, must obviously know the deceased, well, at least one of them, and was obviously protesting too much. A hasty search of the village archives showed that she and her husband had been seen to have a loud disagreement over her winning a goldfish at the previous years' village fair, and him promptly swallowing it. Thus it was obvious she could be the guilty party seeking vengeance for losing her prize to her husband. By mutual agreement they decided to let rest the identity of the second corpse, who they feared might have a brother also in the enforcement trade.

Once the mud had settled, and the third judge to be appointed to the village to hear the case had survived the initial courts proceedings without serious loss of faculties, it was found that no motive, method, or perpetrator could be named. The coroner's report, carefully written over many a jar in the local hostelry, described how the two deceased, drunk as skunks, had attempted to dive into the river, they being as ignorant as Jimmy-the-Cosh about the drought, thus bringing about their own demise.

The time spent arguing for and against everything gave Jimmy time to collect all his betting IOU's and dispose of them. To solidify his defense, should he ever need one, he comforted, courted, and eventually moved in with the bookmaker's widow, so that she, should she ever harbor suspicions over his role in the sudden departure to the hereafter of her husband, could not testify against him. He also inherited the bookie's business, as he said, to help a poor widow woman continue to earn enough honest money to keep the law from her door. By living up to his name he also saved expenses by not needing to hire an enforcer.

Heidi and the Sikh

India in the eighteen-hundreds.
"Prime your gun," the artillery officer barked. "Fire!"
A nineteenth century British cannon needed a dozen men. Two gunners, six soldiers, and four artillery officers.

Skip Winters tucked an unopened letter under his laptop, imagination churning as his fiancée pulled up a chair beside him. "How's your search coming along?"

He breathed deeply to banish the pictures in his mind.

"I traced the family back to Lady Adelaide's arrival in this country six generations back, in 1858."

"Cool."

"Adelaide, Lady Dornside, married twice, both in England. Strangely, using her maiden name each time."

"Did you find anything about her living in India? I thought there was some sort of legend about her?"

"Legends can disguise the truth."

Where to start? With the Honorable British East India Company who fielded its own army and appointed political agents to rule India for the British Crown or with the Indian army mutiny of 1852?

"I traced the East India Company and regimental records through the Internet."

"And?"

"Adelaide really was married to the political agent's aide, an army captain. Before any army unrest surfaced he was ordered to the Punjab to sound out Jat Sikh royalty, a bunch of princes. She went with him."

While he carried out military and political duties, she lived her own lonely social life.

"The official account records the incident in detail. She overheard a Sikh plotting to mutiny, was caught and held hostage."

"Great."

"And praised for having her dog Heidi carry a message to her husband."

"Go on. This is cool."

"The Captain rescued her and sent her back to England to avoid the possible war. The Sikh was executed for treason."

"That's really cool. The family legend *is* true."

"Not quite. In England she had a son, married a man thirty years older, and they moved to America. Her new husband died about two years later. She never had any other children."

"How—?"

Skip held up a hand. "The genealogy back to when she arrived in the country was fairly straightforward. I also went through a trunk in the attic. Don't think anyone's ever searched it."

"So, tell me, what?"

"A scrapbook. Notes of her travels. Official photographs. Mostly innocent."

"What about the dog?"

"There's no record of a dog, except for the one in Lady Adelaide's portrait. I believe it was added later. It's a Wire-haired Dachshund. They were not bred until the end of the 19th century."

"You're saying it's forged?"

He stared at his hands for several moments.

"The record's been cleverly doctored. I believe someone created the legend to protect her reputation."

"How did you work that out?"

"I found a letter. With a poem."

"Go on."

"The Sikhs in the Punjab were loyal to the British. I don't think she overheard anything. I believe the Sikh told her."

"You mean. . . they were friends?"

Why else a poem?

"Possibly more. She still had to warn her husband. To be credible, she'd have to admit how she found out. A liaison with a Sikh would create a scandal, and end her marriage."

"So her husband sent Adelaide home."

"Then executed the Sikh for mutiny."

Justice, revenge, cover up?

"My God. The Brits killed him just for *her* reputation?"

"The family reputation. I don't think she knew. Not then, anyway."

"Didn't the Sikh tell them he was innocent?"

"There's nothing recorded."

"How did they. . . firing squad?"

Much worse.

"They shot him, yes," he said.

The Sikh was blown from a gun. Strapped with the small of his back over the muzzle of a cannon and blasted to bits. Twelve men to kill one.

"What happened to her husband?"

"He died."

Some idiot loaded the cannon with grape shot instead of a blank charge. It severely wounded many of the witnesses, including her husband.

"Her husband lost his leg. It got infected. He died shortly after. As far as I can discover, while his wife was still at sea."

"Did she say anything when she arrived in England?"

"Nothing. She was considered a war widow."

"Think her new husband was paid off?"

"Possibly, but she would have been well off. Her first husband was in government service and few working for the Honorable East India Company were poor. Corruption, or taking advantage of the situation, was expected and accepted. Most made themselves fabulously wealthy."

"Do you think she loved him, her second husband?"

"He gave her a name, then like many family embarrassments, they were sent to the colonies."

"Eighteen-fifty-eight. We weren't a colony then."

"You know what I mean."

"There's something more, isn't there."

"The letter was in Urdu or Punjabi. I couldn't read it. The only parts translated are quotations from a poet, Ghalib, written down the side of the page."

"A love poem?"

"You judge."

'The prison of life and the bondage of grief
are one and the same.
Before the onset of death,
how can man expect to be free of grief?'

"Ghalib didn't distinguish between life and death. He believed that only in death did a lover truly live. Her lover must have believed it too."

'Love knows no difference between life and
death.'

Losing your life for a cause makes you a martyr. Sacrificing your life for another's reputation takes courage beyond belief. Or a great love.

"She didn't translate the rest?"

"Probably didn't want others to read it."

"Did you find a name?"

"The one in the letter matches that of the executed man." He paused a moment. "She gave birth to her son in England."

"With her new husband?"

"She already had him by then."

"She was pregnant when she returned to England?"

Skip said nothing.

"Whose was it? You think the Sikh . . . ?"

"I'm not sure yet."

"Oh my God. That means . . . ."

"I have to tell your father. He is so proud of your family line."

She spun his chair round, catching him off guard, and sat on his knee. She held his face away from her. "You silly boy." She pulled him close and kissed him. "Daddy's thrilled you come from aristocracy, even if they were British, and now you could be descended from a prince—royalty—cool."

"Of his illegitimate son."

"The Sikh could be your grandfather. Well, six back. He helped the British, died for love, and started your family here. You should be proud."

He grinned sheepishly. "Possibly started. Don't jump the gun. Ouch. I didn't mean that."

"Adelaide was a single mom. It's so now."

He shrugged.

"Question. After you found the legend in the company records, why did you keep searching?"

He nodded. "I found something else. There definitely was no dog. "

"What?"

"They hid the secret behind a non-existent dog."

"What was Heidi?"

"Heidi isn't a dog's name; it's also a short form of Adelaide."

"Wow!"

He drew out the envelope from under his laptop. "This is the analysis of my genome. I asked them to look for Indian genetic markers from the male line."

"What does it say?"

He paused briefly, and then he slit it open.

The Transformation of Marmaduke

Marmaduke, a man sturdy of rump and portly of belly, having reached the age of fifty, found himself in a mental quagmire of confusion about his existence. Relating to others had always proved difficult. Now, facing the accelerating descent on the other side of life's hill, and perplexed about his role in the grand scheme of things, he did what many of his age do, he decided to take up pastimes that he had passed by on his journey, hoping that fresh experiences might provide insight into his problem.

Sports cars and motorcycles held no appeal, attracted, as he found himself, to a more natural life, one shared by the majority of plants and creatures on the planet and mainly ignored by those he did not relate to.

So it was that one morning found him galloping blithely along on a horse, the breeze in his hair, what was left of it, and the smells of the countryside in his nostrils, reveling in a communion with his newfound love of the great outdoors. His imagination gave him no forewarning of danger when he ducked under a tree branch, which as fate would have it, sported a stout snag on its underside which hooked in the rider's belt and hoisted him from his mount.

Dangling in space he watched the rump of his horse disappear into the future.

He swung gently.

An exploring squirrel chanced upon the belt, and not comprehending what it was that dangled beneath him, and thus quite unalarmed, nibbled at the leather intrigued by the smell.

Marmaduke sensed this interference with his clothing, and suspicious that something, anything, might chew through his only support and precipitate him in a downward trajectory, tried to screw his head around to see who would dare to do such a thing. This startled the unsuspecting rodent which leaped straight up in the air. Forgetting to grab at the branch on its downward path, having once reached the pinnacle of his upward flight, it missed the branch and landed on Marmaduke's rump, thus causing similar consternation in both of nature's creatures.

The squirrel did an about face and scrambled back to the safety of the trunk.

A few minutes passed before the squirrel, being a curious creature, decided to re-explore the cause of its sudden fright and crawled, gingerly, in fits and starts, as squirrels are wont to do, back toward Marmaduke's gently swinging rump where it decided to rest, the rump being softer than the branch. It retrieved a nut from its cheek pouch and chewed, ruminating on the strange turn of events so early in the morning. Actually, it was early for Marmaduke, mid-morning for the furry critter.

Reassured that the small furry beast intended no harm, Marmaduke tried his chances as a squirrel whisperer, he having little else to do but swing, and the rodent being his only immediate companion.

His speech was arrested when he spied a long snake, which he estimated at several yards in length—although his calculation may have been a little off, he having lost his glasses when he parted with his horse—which slithered toward the tree and began a sinuous climb.

This raised serious doubts in Marmaduke's mind as to the sensibility of dangling helpless from a tree branch, his rump a chance bistro for the squirrel, and himself a potential prey for a snake.

Once it reached the level of the branch where the luckless pair was lodged, the serpent turned its attention toward them, and preceded by its flicking tongue, continued to slither its sinuous way toward them. This of course Marmaduke could only imagine, since he could not raise his head sufficiently to view the herpetic advance.

His life was in the hands of his imagination, which rose to the occasion.

To avoid the snake he must descend to the ground. The fate of the squirrel was now bound to his, as its only path back to the main trunk of the tree was blocked by the slitherer.

Being suspended from his belt, from a point almost at his center of gravity, gave him the idea to swing his body and attempt to grasp the branch with his hands. This proved quite impossible to do as he could not quite lift his arms far enough above to reach the branch. He felt a sense of scorn from the squirrel.

His legs were another matter, although he felt that tipping his head forward to raise his legs might undo his belt from the offending spur. His imagination in overdrive, he decided to try, as he knew the snake would reach them both before long, and although he expected the snake to first attend to the squirrel, thus providing him with a little more time, he felt a bond with the little critter sitting on his rump, and allowing him to be eaten to spare his own life seemed disloyal, Marmaduke being nothing if not a man of strong and loyal convictions, once a friendship had been established.

As he swung his body, he felt the tiny sharp claws dig into his behind.

On the third attempt he managed to hook both legs over the branch and lock his ankles together. Bending his knees, he pulled with his legs, dislodged the belt from its restraint on the wooden spur, and found himself dangling upside down by his feet with a frantic little squirrel clinging to him for dear life.

Remembering diving lessons from forced swimming sessions in a bygone age, lessons he had avoided whenever possible, he considered whether he had enough time to drop, tuck and somersault before meeting the ground, to avoid landing on his head. By this time all possibility of mathematical calculations escaped his semi-frozen brain.

The squirrel probably felt the same way.

Still, hanging by his feet he thought he might be able to bend his body, reach up and grasp the branch with his hands. This he did. His hands closed over a cold slippery body which he barely had time to register as the snake before he reflexively released his grip, and he and the squirrel plummeted the few feet—horses not being very tall—to the ground, to the sound of crunching glass as he descended feet first on his eye-glasses, then fell to one knee.

The snake, obviously disturbed by their encounter, also released its hold on the branch and fell beside him.

All three stared at one another; the snake apparently puzzled, Marmaduke myopically, and the squirrel in disbelief.

A fleeting thought that he wished his furry friend was a mongoose who could take on the snake in honorable battle was banished when he focused on how close together they were. Close enough in fact to see the reptile's eyes. Poisonous snakes had elliptical pupils didn't they? But not coral snakes. As he looked at their dangerous companion, that's how he now thought of it, and he felt sure the squirrel did too, it slithered away before he really looked in its eyes, which he felt was just as well. What if he had frozen like a rat—or a squirrel?

He climbed to his feet. The squirrel firmly gripping his shoulder, walked to the tree, sat down, and leaned against the trunk. Of the snake, there was no sign. He put his hand to his shoulder, but his little companion had disappeared.

About to start for home, on two legs, the four legged mount having long since disappeared over the horizon, he felt a tug on the leg of his jeans. His little furry companion had returned and was climbing slowly over his leg. Marmaduke watched in fascination as the little critter reached into its mouth, disgorged an acorn and laid it gently in his lap.

Marmaduke knew with certainty that his little friend had brought forth a gift in thanks, and that he was expected to eat it, squirrel saliva and all, when the thought overwhelmed him that with one bite of the nut he would be privy to the knowledge of life. He glanced down to reassure himself he wore jeans and would have no need of a fig leaf. His expectation of learning was short lived, as the branch from which he had dangled, fortunately away from the view of others, decided to yield to the stress recently placed on it by the animal trio, broke from the trunk, and fell on Marmaduke's head.

The recovery of his faculties after regaining consciousness was complicated by a hospital environment — someone, unknown, had apparently found him—because he and the medical staff seemed at odds over his explanation for his predicament., they being firmly of the opinion that he had fallen from the tree while collecting acorns, with the evidence that he had been chewing one when found, and he constantly asking whether he had been sporting a fig-leaf.

His story of his airborne suspension while communing with animals was treated with the seriosity only medical staff can bring to bear on an explanation of which they are sincerely skeptical, and his inability to produce evidence or witnesses to confirm his story.

Once on the medical road to recovery, the staff in a unanimous decision moved him to a psych ward, not least of the reasons being his insistence on making faces at a squirrel that sat each morning on the sill outside his window laying a line of nuts as if counting them.

The following morning a nurse made so bold to open the window to provide a fresh-air treatment, that being in vogue at the time. She was later found, having fainted on the floor, apparently at the sight of a squirrel snuggled in the crook of Marmaduke's neck, a snake curled up in repose at the foot of the bed, and a horse with its head through the window holding a broken pair of eye glasses in its mouth.

The Drawing

I had not expected the past to be thrust so rudely in my face.

Young ardent troops carried clipboards bearing the name of the Mayor, fighting for the old school building as a standard of their past, a cause they thought they understood, expecting signatures as if it were their right. Some wore costumes of a bygone southern era, one they could not relinquish.

The flag had yielded to pressure. A bitter pill to swallow. Before it could be torn down they had lowered it, and hidden it in a place of reverence; a safe place, away from protestors.

Now they had drawn the battle line for their last stand.

The statue in the circle out front of the school, a mounted Confederate colonel, arm raised before a charge, still stood. Despite the pride and courage cast in the bronze, his attack had led to death and disaster. His statue was the true focus of the fight, with their petition aimed at the historic significance of the school to mask their adulation of the mythic and long dead colonel.

He carried a name still revered in the town.

"It is part of our heritage," she said—a young girl, no more than fifteen, with an eager, glowing face that stirred unbidden memories.

She had forsworn jeans or shorts in favor of a hooped skirt, the more to impress us with her message, but only fine ladies of the era wore such dresses. The war was fought by many more who could barely afford a change of clothes, let alone the five yards of fabric for such a flouncy gown—when it could be smuggled from the mills in the north.

Humidity beaded the sweat on her forehead. Blotches on the page she carried showed where wayward drops had missed the wipe of her kerchief. It didn't interfere with the innocence of her smile. The social attitude had changed little since the Civil War. Progress was acceptable, but not at the expense of the tarnished past.

I ran my left hand over my thinning hair, where a round monk-like bald patch sat like a yarmulke pretending to defend me against the sun.

"Some say this past is best forgotten," I told her.

"You can sign your name here." She indicated a line below a list of names.

I looked down at her. At her age, a late bloomer, I had probably been no taller.

I saw her hesitation as she glanced at my hands.

"Or I can write it for you," she said.

She averted her gaze from the nubs emerging from my palm where fingers had once been, enough left that I had been able to retrain them to hold a pencil or pen. Being taken by surprise I had not had time to wear a glove to spare her embarrassment, or questions best avoided.

"That won't be necessary"

She waited expectantly.

"Let the developers have it."

Her smile was replaced with eyes opened a little wider in surprise. How could any man in the south ignore such a request? Or follow a belief other than the cause she represented. Her expression slowly changed from disbelief to disgust.

Her knowledge of local history probably ended in 1865. She knew nothing of the school in the twentieth century; in the past sixty years, or of the passion which swept me up in the mid-nineteen fifties, sixty years before.

"We have been educated in a school house here since 1850," she said, as if that should finalize the argument. "It is part of our identity."

She waited as if expecting me to sign despite the exchange. "I just need a signature. Everyone has signed."

"The mayor is leading the fight?"

"My great uncle? Yes. He lives in a different part of town." She spoke as if I, Manolo, didn't know that. She could have added away from the poorer members of society, in a gated community of the affluent, away from the artists that had gradually swelled the community during the last few years.

At last she accepted my refusal.

"Damn Yankee!" She would have stomped her foot, but despite her dress and convictions, she did not carry the repertoire of gestures of a Southern Belle.

I would have smiled, had the memory not been so painful. This was the town of my birth.

I had rented a house for a week after being invited to receive an award. Two of my drawings hung in the Capital. My first time back in sixty years, I had not come without trepidation. Would I be recognized? And if so. . . .

But this was a journey I had put off for too long. One I knew I must eventually make. We must all learn to face down the bitterness of the past, unless we wish to carry it like a festering wound to the grave.

* * *

I had been at odds with others in this town before. My classmates—dare I call them that—thought that a father who repaired shoes for a living, and a mother a maid, was grounds for incessant teasing. I perched low on the class totem, barely visible to others unless I challenged their standing.

In the new school year of 1955, the class had started art lessons. They knew nothing of my parent's efforts to buy pencils, or my efforts to save them to the least little stub, or of my drawings. Instead they seized on my ability as if I were an alien invading their private world.

"How did you draw this?"

"You copied this."

"You stole this."

"Who heard of a poor boy like you drawing?"

"You should help your father nail shoes; it's all you are both good for."

I existed on the periphery of the class. How dare I draw better than they?

And I was not expected to fall in love.

Unprepared, I had the temerity to love the one girl in the class who could have been a Belle. Even her name told of it, Sarah.

I tried to approach her once while the semester was still young, and we were yet to have a drawing test. My interest was noted and my pencil study of the Virgin Mary sprouted a moustache and crude pendulous breasts. I tore up the defaced drawing and failed the assignment.

The message was clear. In their company, I must not succeed, so I produced drawings without merit for class consumption. My private drawings, no one saw.

"Damn Yankee." At her voice, the memories surged into consciousness like overripe bile. And the pain.

Young and naive, smitten by the early adolescent rush of passion, and unable to approach her, I left small presents, without a name, in her desk, or close by where she would know they were for her. But after a while she held them aloft and told the class of her secret admirer. Rumor-mongers tried to uncover the lucky one who sought her favors among the class favorites; beaus who could never claim the role, but likewise never denied it.

Unlike her beauty, her drawing talent was mediocre. Perhaps I could show my adoration by secretly improving her drawings. Sneaking into school after hours, I retouched her drawings—a catch-light in the eye here, subtle shading there, here the inner corners of the eyes accentuated, an ear lobe more defined.

Soon she was accepted as among the best artists in the class. If she knew the reason, she said nothing, and accepted the glory. But although she basked in the adoration, she was never passionate about art. This was as painful as her ignoring me.

As the weeks passed I was caught by my own cleverness. If I stopped my secret support, her art would revert to the humdrum, her reputation sullied. For me to stop would expose her true mediocrity to the class. Then a school patron announced a cruel trap; the winner of a drawing contest, as judged by an outside panel of local artists, would be granted a scholarship to study art.

Her admirers expected Sarah to win. If I withdrew my help the judging could precipitate a scandal. My help would simply defer the inevitable exposure.

The night before the judging her two brothers stumbled late into the classroom. I believed they had been drinking in anticipation of her success. My hands held the remains of her entry. It was for her sake. They did not believe it.

The sound of the paper guillotine still rings in my head, slicing through my fingers, hesitating only briefly when it met bone, until her brother slammed his hand on the handle and the fingers fell away like slim cocktail sausages devoid of feeling. They did not touch my left hand, one should teach me, or perhaps they couldn't stand the screams, even against the gag. And they left my thumb alone.

I had only tried to save her from embarrassment.

It was a stupid accident, I said, but I left the school abruptly, before too many questions, and had never returned—until now.

* * *

Expecting another harangue about my failure to sign, I put on my glove and opened the door when the girl in crinoline came back the following day, reminding me again of an angel climbed down from a crèche.

Instead she smiled. "I have a message from my Grandmother," she said, passing me an envelope. It held a short letter and a pressed flower from the past.

I thought I always knew, she wrote, about everything, but was terrified to speak up because of what they would have done to you. But your hand . . .

I found it hard to see past the stinging sensation in my eyes.

"I still will not sign," I said.

"I am not sure what happened," Miss Crinoline said. "I heard her arguing with my uncle after I told her of your hand. She made him withdraw the petition." Her face registered her bewilderment for a lost cause.

I glanced at a postscript and crumpled up the note before I read it again. She said she would be at the ceremony. After so many years, I doubted I would recognize her, or she, me.

Looking at the past is like looking at history through a kaleidoscope, swirls and colors defying reality. The physical part of it would always remain in the present, but I could not retouch life.

I felt the young girl's hand on my arm. She held out a print of one of my studies, as if to tell me she knew about me without using words.

Expressions of wonder and confusion co-mingled on her face.

"You must have loved her very much." Her eyes glistened. "Do you still?"

Sometimes there is no right answer.

The Riverboat

"Ram Baba gives you his blessing my son." The bearded guru intoned the few words of Urdu he'd learned at The Punjab Grill, touched Mick's shoulder with a peacock feather and handed him a flower. "Go in peace."

"Seamus," Mick said. "It *is* you hiding under those robes. Mother of God, what are you up to now? I've been looking all over for you."

"Hush, my son." The Guru leaned forward. His head touched that of the man kneeling before him. "Keep your voice down. Cabin 460, ten minutes, deck four."

Minutes later Mick entered the guru's cabin, walked over to the balcony, and gazed at the river. "It's wicked dark tonight."

"How did you find me? I thought you were out of my life forever." Seamus peeled away the beard, revealing the scars of his teenage acne. He threw it on the dresser, reached into a small fridge, and grabbed two beers.

"When did you, a mortal sinner, become a guru?" Mick said over his shoulder.

Seamus handed him a beer. "Mafia Mick. Still the strong arm man keeping up parish attendance for Father Murphy and sharing the offerings with yourself?" he asked, scrubbing his face free of spirit gum.

"It's hardly a living. But look at you, Ram Baba. You sound like a sticky dessert." Mick swept his arm toward the furnishings, "and just as rich. How did you con the Captain to let you operate on a casino boat?"

"He knows a good game when he sees it. We're partners. This way the patrons can gamble on salvation, spiritual and financial."

"Seamus Malone, are you even still religious? Didn't you get the boot from Father Murphy?"

"Thanks to you."

"You were short on the donations too often."

"Mick, you evil devil, he blamed me for your losses."

Mick grinned. "The confessional is a powerful tool for mis-communication."

"Is that so?" Seamus let the words drip out as he digested Mike's comment. "Confession. I didn't think of that."

"What do *you* really give them for the money?" Seamus paused and stared at his old buddy.

"The hope they're looking for, here and now, and for the hereafter. The blessing might rub off in the casino, too. They don't understand an Irish-Indian accent. It sounds important. And I give them each a flower as a mark of spiritual respect."

"They give you money, and you give them zip. You fraud."

"I thought that once. Now I see they do believe. So, they give generously. You saw my limo. I have a yacht as well."

"You owe me fifty bucks. I had to pay to see you."

"It's a lot more than $50 you'd need to get salvation from me."

"Don't friends get a discount with the forgiveness?" Mick said. "For old times' sake."

"Friends? I'm still thinking of your *confession* to father Murphy."

"Business is business. I needed the money. But you're doing very well for yourself." He grinned at Seamus. "And if I hadn't arranged your *resignation*, you would never have started this scheme."

"So I have to thank you for showing me religion can be profitable?"

"Fancy, taking your first steps in larceny in a church. Hey, what's happening?"

"We're under way. Now it's dark, we cruise the river for a few hours."

"Do you have another blessing tonight?"

"Usually, but you're here, so I'll give it a miss." He thrust his arms into the sleeves of a black shirt and pulled it over his head. "What were you saying? You needed the money, and rewarded me with the heave-ho. No, you maneuvered Father Murphy to do your dirty work." Seamus paused for a moment. "Why are you really here?"

"Things are tight. The old way doesn't work like it used to. Takings are down."

"And you're looking for a donation."

"Listen to you. Working on a casino boat, having your own yacht, you need a lifeguard," said Mick. "The river's a dangerous place. Think of me as—insurance."

Seamus stared at him. "It used to be called protection."

"Whatever."

"A shakedown."

"Seamus, we're mates. Share the burden and the take. Like we used to."

"You think?"

"Man, that casino is noisy. I'm not sure I'd like that part of it."

"I love it. It's the sound of belief and hope." Seamus joined his visitor on the balcony.

"Where are we?" Mick asked.

"The middle of the river. Hard to see anything on a night this dark, but those lights way over there, that's the far shore."

Mick looked out over the balcony rail. "We have it made."

"We?"

"Seamus my man, I'm sure you have a place for me. I mean, what would your clients think if they heard about your past? Not that I'm saying...."

Seamus stared at him sharply. "So, that's the way it is?"

"I knew you'd understand. Let's drink to our partnership."

"You're right. I have a career to protect."

"Which we do not intend to give up."

"We? No indeed." Seamus hesitated a moment, then bent down as if to tie a shoe lace. "You a lifeguard? You don't even swim." Grasping Mick's trouser legs at the ankles, he straightened and heaved. He barely heard the splash over the sound of the wind.

He moved into the cabin. Standing in front of the mirror he tapped himself on both shoulders with the feather. He felt nothing, so he repeated it, and recited the Urdu incantation he used for his believers. He pursed his lips and frowned.

"Damn. It's the confessional for you me lad—insurance as Mick would say—like the old days. Though, I'd better hide the limo. If Father Murphy sees that, he might want in on the deal—as penance for my sins of course."

The Pickup

Ian fidgeted on the wall of the bridge. Would his evening end no better philosophically than it began? Dee-Dee's fall had sealed his fate. Saving her once dictated that he rescue her now, although he couldn't swim.

Whirlpools of thought matched the turbulent river below. Memories and intentions, competed with the certainty of his demise if he tried to save her. He remembered how, at the age of seven, he had watched his hat float away to be lost forever in the harbor at Port Sudan while he sank below the surface—before his father rose from the water in front of him, his bald head glistening like a pale apple, and towed him to safety—and being unable to interest anyone in retrieving it. Dee-Dee was more than a hat!

Dee-Dee had floated further away. One arm rose and fell, beating the surface of the water. Showers of droplets reflected the light from the street-lamps lining the bridge, a sparkling backdrop to her pallid face.

How macabre, that in this situation, building inexorably to its climax, he recalled memories long suppressed. Much like, he supposed, one re-lives one's life when drowning. Although if one lived to tell the story, one had not drowned! What were Dee-Dee's thoughts?

He shielded his eyes from the glare of the lamplight to better witness the tableau in which he, an unwilling participant, now found himself.

How did she feel? Did it matter? Did that influence what he must decide?

The evening had begun badly. It was a dark and stormy night when, seeking shelter, they had met in the smoky opacity of the party. Her eyes, liquid pools of fear and longing, appealed for help—her dress, too tight for underwear, too sheer for modesty, exposed her glistening bust, in danger of joining the canapés of her plate, that, with a half-empty glass, filled her hands—to dislodge the skewer of the shish-kabob impaled in the gap between her front teeth, the sharp point buried in her tongue, holding her mouth open and frustrating her cries for help.

That thin sliver of bamboo, an assegai in the hand of fate, had speared their psyches together. Their eyes talked, understanding the language preceding speech. Through gesture, the touch of fingertips, the brush of skin on skin, they learned, each of the other.

Her fall had not been intentional, unless directed by a supernatural hand. Exuberance that cast aside care, relief at her earlier rescue, Ian's fusion with her aura, their same Scotch, their same cigarettes, whirled them together in the now misty rain glistening the stone and concrete even as their souls glistened. Dee-Dee had danced along the wall, and slipped into the waters that haunted his past.

Pulling from her teeth the kebab which threatened her life meant he now owned that life, and obligated his further action. He squirmed, anxious to resolve existential questions that had lain dormant or ignored, like his memories of partial drowning, as he looked at the water below.

Why were they here?

Is there a real me?

Is there a beyond?

The school of existential philosophy claimed everything was in the mind. Belief and reality were mental phenomena constructed by the mind of a living breathing human, even to the creation of God.

He didn't understand the philosophical reasoning.

I am aware, he thought. How does the *me* relate to the character this body exhibits, dictated by a random mix of genes at conception? Could that chromosome-derived personality continue after death? Would they meet beyond?

What if God really was a philosophical creation as the nineteenth century philosophers claimed, merely an idea like the ones now intruding on his plight?

He caught a glimpse of Dee-Dee's hair floating on the surface, a fading halo, a remnant of her being resting on the choppy surface of the water. Her arm had disappeared, her face no longer visible. Was she still real? Dare he abandon her to join other abandoned heroines who littered the pages of history, great love springing from the roots of tragedy?

He made his decision. In his mind, Ian jumped to join her.

It was so purely existential.

Two

He had once been known as Juan, a teacher helping children. Now he could help no one except his only friend, a dog, as homeless as he.

Old and bearded, his ragged shirt hanging over torn pants tied round his waist with string, he smelled of urine and cast off clothing. The laces had fallen from the ripped holes on the top of his shoes, lost, perhaps in the gutter. Since the mudslide that wiped away all he once lived for, he had squatted everyday in city doorways where he could shelter from the rain, holding a can as bent and wrinkled as himself, hoping for a coin to buy the next meal. Most people hurried by without looking at him.

He shared his loneliness with a coarse-haired hound and his memories, shrunk to a few isolated scenes, like photographs pinned to a corkboard of his life, separated by blank areas of forgetfulness. The dog leaned against him, trailing a rope from its skinny neck.

One morning, a little girl tugged herself free of a woman's hand as they passed. She stopped to stare at the man as very young children will. He looked up at her with a smile, crooked and stained, with gaps where teeth had once been. She gazed back, her face solemn, head bent forward, peering shyly from under long lashes, as if sorry for something she might have done, and doubting her own innocence.

She held out her hand, a cookie in her fingers, the edges ragged from her teeth and damp with saliva. The direction of her gaze told him it was for his dog.

The woman dragged the child away. The girl glanced up at her, then at the man in the doorway with his dog, and threw the cookie to him. The woman hustled her to a waiting car where a driver in uniform, as crisp as the winter morning, took her umbrella. He held it aloft and opened the car door. The woman thanked him in English, then she and the quiet child climbed in.

The bearded man who smelled of urine had not eaten in two days, but he broke the cookie and gave most to his dog, who sniffed, then gently bit at the softened edges as if it knew they must share and eat slowly to make it last. The man chewed what was left.

He pulled a small photograph from his pocket, the wrinkles in the paper ageing the face that smiled back. His eyes moistened with memories. Fingers deeply stained and ending in nails chewed to the quick, smoothed the creases, and the face grew young again. A wet drop fell on it, though whether from the rain or from his eyes he was not sure. It didn't matter. He wiped the photograph against his shirt.

Instead of the solemn little girl who had stopped beside him, the face in the photograph glowed with life barely begun. He had not bought her a puppy because he had not thought it important. By the time he understood, she had been taken. He had been unable to rewrite the past.

He had seen the woman and her crisp driver before. She had passed his doorway many times, like so many others, as if he and his dog did not exist. The little girl he had never seen.

On the next day, and the next, the woman dragged the little girl past his squatting place toward the car. The little one looked at him from under her sad eyelids and no one said a word.

By the fourth day he felt the heaviness of the silence between them. This time she stopped again. She strained against the woman's hand toward the dog. The dog pulled against his own restraint, its tongue lolling, and the white tip to its black tail beating time to secret thoughts.

The little girl looked at the dog, but the woman would not let her touch it, and the man wondered why.

"He is safe," he said.

The little girl said nothing. The woman said her granddaughter had not spoken since her parents were taken. He knew what she meant, loss being a tragedy they shared.

On the next day, the man who had been a teacher told the child his dog's name was Two. She didn't reply. "Because I am Juan," he said, and smiled at his own English joke. She reached out her hand. The dog licked it and morning sunshine spread over her face. She smiled at the dog, then at her grandmother, and the dog licked her fingers again.

On the fifth day she laughed as Two licked her fingers. Her grandmother gasped and hugged her, but she pulled away and leaned toward the dog.

"That is the first time she has laughed since..." the woman said.

The man, who had been known as Juan, held out the end of the dog's rope to them both. "She must have the dog," he said. "He has fleas. You can clean him."

"But he is yours," the woman said. "Why?"

"Because," he said, and shrugged. "Every child should have a dog."

When they had gone he looked at his crumpled photograph. He knew she would approve. He could not let the dog see him again in case it wanted to return. In the afternoon he found another doorway where the woman and the little girl and Two would not find him, but it was not so sheltered and he felt the chill.

Late in the winter, fever struck him. A city van picked up his body to carry it to the mortuary, but he still breathed so instead it took him to the Sisters of Mercy. They cleaned him, exorcized the smell of urine, trimmed his ragged beard and laid him in a bed with a clean nightshirt, the crumpled photograph placed like an icon on the small locker beside his bed. The man lay thinking of a little girl, sometimes not knowing which one, aware he had begun his final contest with the quiet release spreading through his body. He knew he would never again sit in a doorway with his only friend, a dog who had brought laughter to a little girl.

That's where the woman and her granddaughter found him.

The little girl came close to the bed and stared at him in her solemn way.

"Two," she said.

"I have come to thank you," her grandmother said. "She has started to speak again, to her dog, and sometimes to us."

He smiled through the tiredness that would soon separate them forever.

"What can I call you?" his voice a whisper, like the breeze blowing through the window.

"Angela," she said.

He repeated it to himself, leaving off the final A.

Her grandmother thanked again the man who had once been a teacher, and he smiled.

When they left, he held the wrinkled photograph so he could see the young face. As he watched, the creases dissolved for the last time.

He lay, arms crossed, still smiling, holding the photograph, when a sister pulled up the sheet over his body.

I am Oliver, and I am a Cat

I felt I should give the last word to Oliver. He is my feline mentor, advisor, and all round patriarch on whom I rely for the paw of approval, and at fifteen he deserves to be honored as a patriarch, as I am honored to be a member of his family. And, I well remember what I learned years ago, a cat can communicate most effectively when it deigns to.

"If your pets could write about you, what do you think they would say?" He was lecturing me in the interval between my awakening and filling his food dish. This was obviously a direct challenge for me to ask what *he* would say.

"You'd have to tame a cockroach to write for you, like Mehitabel has," I replied, trying to confuse him.

"I don't need an Archie, I have you."

"Touché." I paused a second, after all I still wasn't quite awake. "How do you know about Archie and Mehitabel?"

"I am Oliver, and I am a cat. As you should know, that makes me omniscient. I can trace my family back to the ancient Gods of Egypt. Can you say the same?"

"Well, they had to be ancient in those days, didn't they?" He glared at me and scooped up another piece of food with his paw. I gave in. "So what would you say?"

He carefully chewed and swallowed before replying.

"My owner loves me; he would do anything for me, as long as my tail is cut off, my ears cropped for his vanity, my toes declawed. Oh, and he cut my balls off."

"Oliver! No one has touched your ears and tail."

"I speak for all pets," he said, with a condescending tilt of his head.

"If you speak for all pets," I replied, "Perhaps you should say, 'She stayed by me in the hurricane and risked her life for me? Or he shares my food because he cannot afford anything else, and he will not abandon me.'" I thought I had him there because he ignored me, so I went on. "During Hurricane Katrina, FEMA, the Federal Emergency Management Agency, didn't allow people to take their animals with them. Half of those who stayed behind in New Orleans did so because they wouldn't abandon their pets, even when their own lives were in severe danger."

He sniffed. I had obviously bested him with that reply, so he ignored me.

"My direct ancestor Mafdet was the first Egyptian feline goddess," he said. It was if I hadn't spoken. "But the most famous was Bastet. She was not only a household goddess, protector of women, children and domestic cats, but she was also the goddess of sunrise, music, dance, pleasure, as well as family, fertility and birth."

"She needed her God-like powers to prevent being overwhelmed with obligations," I quipped.

"Don't be facetious. Anyway, she made sure that the penalty for killing a cat—even accidentally—was death. If a house caught on fire, the cats were rescued before the people, just as it should be!"

"Not all Egyptian Gods were cats. What about Anubis?"

"That jackal-headed dog? Elevating him to divine status was idiotic. But that happened before they realized that the *first cat* was the daughter of Isis, and the goddess for the moon and the sun. They even, very wisely I might add, built a whole city for cat worship, Bubastis, in honor of Bastet."

"So why did medieval Europeans believe cats were in league with the Devil?" I said. "Cats were burned along with witches."

"Some of *your* ancestors weren't so bright."

"Wasn't Bubastis that depraved place where thousands of pilgrims sang silly songs, drank wine, prayed, and showed their wild behavior at an annual Bubastis Oktoberfest?"

Again he ignored my comments.

"Unfortunately, this city was destroyed by the unthinking Persians in 350 BC," he said.

"You left us with a dubious legacy. Young humans have adopted the behavior of Bastet's worshippers. We call it *Spring Break.*"

His tail twitched reflecting possible annoyance despite his outward appearance of calm control.

"In America, in 2009, I admit we at last recognized that our relationship to our pets, to you, had undergone a profound change," I said. "We are no longer merely *owners.*"

"You never have been." He sounded a little petulant. "At least not where we cats are concerned."

"May I remind you that we let your more recent ancestors into our homes? We of all the animal species have developed a close relationship with other species. We have created the human-animal bond."

"The animal-human bond was a mutual arrangement. But it is often bondage—for the animal. Some you keep in bondage to raise for food; some to work. And some you support only for vanity. Those are the ones you call pets."

What is a pet? I mused. A pet is a domesticated animal kept for pleasure rather than utility, and we should note that the verb, to pet, expresses fondness, or means to stroke gently or lovingly. It is said that it can also mean a fit of peevishness, sulkiness, or anger. At first I thought that was just propaganda, but after listening to Oliver I was no longer sure.

He went on without waiting for a reply. "Dogs and cats are the only two animals that you let freely into your homes, and allow to become members of your families. Farm animals, birds, or exotic pets are still captives."

Pets do reflect the ying and yang of our special relationship with species other than our own.

They highlight the best and the worst of human behavior. Just as we need ugliness to appreciate beauty, sin to appreciate good, hate to appreciate love, so we need our special relationship to our pets to provide us with a mirror to our own soul. Who of you can you look into their pet's eyes and deny this? I daren't admit this to Oliver. Not just yet.

"We cats domesticated *you*," he said.

"Your ancestors joined us to feed on the vermin in grain silos," I protested.

"They were pests surrounding your homes."

"What?"

"You had a filthy existence until we took over vermin control for you."

"Well, dogs developed a *symbiotic* relationship with us, guarding us and hunting for us in return for food and shelter." I didn't want to add that this relationship is so close that the dog breeds we have so diligently bred cannot exist without human friendship—anymore than we can exist without theirs—but Oliver beat me to it.

"Your family house-cat can fend for itself, hunt for food, and adapt to a wild environment. Can you see a Shi Tzu, Pug, or miniature Yorkie doing the same?"

"You have a point," I conceded.

"And you should bear in mind," he wagged his tail for emphasis. "There are as many feral cats in this country as those in your houses."

"Feral cats are a damn nuisance."

"If you got rid of them, the country would be overrun by rodents."

I quickly changed the subject. I didn't think it polite to talk about trapping his distant relatives. I do have some sensitivity.

"We view our *bond* differently now, and use terms like *companion, guardian,* and *steward,* instead of owner," I said. The loss of human and animal life during Hurricane Katrina had helped us recognize this need.

"On October 6th 2006, President Bush signed the PETS Act (Pets Evacuation and Transportation Standards), into law," I said. "States must have animal evacuation protocols in order to get disaster preparedness funds from FEMA, and allow FEMA to pay for shelters, for both animals and their guardians, in an emergency. "

The Fritz Institute predicted that the PETS Act would save thousands of animal and human lives. It has already. Before hurricane Gustav, the authorities in New Orleans organized the Louisiana Mega Shelter which housed more than 1000 animals—cats, dogs, rabbits, lizards, snakes and turtles. Ninety-five percent of evacuees—1.9 million people—were able to take their pets with them when they left.

Oliver interrupted my train of thought.

"It's time for a nap." He leaped onto the windowsill and gave a grunt meaning I should move things so he could lie in the sun.

"What I do for you," I said.

He stretched, rubbing his face on the sill to claim ownership, and sighed with Tuna baited breath.

"One last thought I might write down for you. I think it's about time you learned the truth about us," he said. "And a bit about dogs. Puppies and Kittens are really alien invaders, sent to subjugate earth. Their role is to win your affection, and overcome you with love. Then the puppies grow into dogs to police you, and the kittens grow into cats to govern you."

The alien thing seemed far-fetched, and I thought I saw him wink, but the rest of what he said had a ring of truth.

"You can leave me now," he said. "It's time for a nap."

I crept away quietly so as not to disturb him. I had to write his thoughts down before I forgot them; after all, although I was letting him have the last word, he doesn't have an Archie.

Other books by Robert Hart:

Available on line at Amazon.com, B&N.com, and all regular book sites.

Cage Liners, Stories about Pets, Vets, owners, and other animals. ISBN# 978-149607596, Published 2015
Oliver's Rubaiyat, A Cat Questions Life. ISBN#978-1492302919, Published 2014

If you enjoyed these stories, please share with your fellow readers by posting a review on Goodreads or Amazon.
You can contact the author at:
upppitywomanpress@gmail.com